DEVOTION'S DAWN

A SHADOW CASTERS SHORT STORY

JARED WOODCOX

CONTENTS

JOIN READERS GROUP

Welcome to the Shadow Casters Universe!

Never miss a new release by signing up for my free Readers Group. Learn of special offers and interesting details that aren't in the books. Go to Shadowcasterseries.com to sign up. You can unsubscribe at any time.

PART ONE
THE HERMIT OF FILLENGLEN

CHAPTER 1

SNOWY ASCENT

Cylos Phetos could hardly feel his fingers. It had been an unusually cold winter in the western mountains of Malgar, and nowhere had been hit harder than the little town of Fillenglen. As if times weren't already dire enough, the bitter winter that had come two months early had devastated the last harvest of the season. Many caught unprepared had seen their homes damaged and left uninhabitable from heavy snowstorms arriving completely unforeseen.

Cylos paused a moment, daring to bend his stiff and numb fingers just enough to slip off his freezing gloves. Gingerly pulling down the scarf he wore over his nose so only his eyes were left uncovered, his brittle fingers felt like they might break off. Exposing his mouth, he brought his aching hands to it, exhaling warm air in a desperate attempt to thaw them out. Somehow even his breath felt cold. He tried his best to ignore stinging eyes that felt like they might freeze solid.

Most boys his age would have never dared to leave the comfort of a home warmed by fire to set out in the treacherous wooded taiga. But Cylos wasn't like other twelve-year-olds. He had a promise to keep and not even the most treacherous bitter cold and frozen terrain could sway him from his commitment.

Belza was expecting him, had entrusted him with this weekly task, and without the precious supplies Cylos carried, there was no guarantee the old man would survive the harsh conditions.

Cylos's mother hadn't wanted him to go, but his father was insistent. This didn't bother Cylos any, quite the opposite. He likely would have sneaked out of his house even if *both* parents had tried to stop him. But he and his father were likeminded. No obstacle was too great to hinder them from keeping their word and maintaining their honor. Cylos would stop at nothing to make his father proud. He looked up to him in every way and strove to always meet his expectations, no matter the risk or discomfort to himself.

Thus, a task others may deem daunting for a young boy felt routine. Cylos considered himself mature beyond his years. He'd been born in an era of severe hardship and had no choice but to grow up quickly. His mother often told him of the storms and famines that decimated Malgar. Or how trade to remote towns like Fillenglen had all but halted, requiring locals to produce everything themselves. Necessities were hard to come by. Luxuries were unheard of.

Thinking about their humble circumstances, Cylos wondered if his own family would survive the bitter winter and tenuous conditions themselves without his weekly exchange of goods. If anything happened to his parents because Cylos had been unwilling to act, he'd never forgive himself. He took pride in pleasing and contributing to his family.

Besides, he'd grown to treasure his friendship with old Belza and enjoyed spending time with him. Cylos didn't know much about the man who had come to build a home in the mountains above Fillenglen early that summer. But from the moment he arrived, Cylos's parents had greeted him warmly and treated him well. Right away Belza and Cylos's father had agreed the boy would visit Belza's cabin once a week for an exchange of supplies, helping sustain both Belza and the Phetos family. Cylos didn't fully understand why his father had assigned his young son the perilous and taxing trek up the mountain, but he didn't ask questions.

Week after week, Cylos made the traverse to Belza's cabin, bearing necessities for the old hermit. The supplies he carried changed based on what his family had available and what Belza needed. This time he carried warm clothing and blankets sewn by his mother, fish caught through the ice from the lake northeast of Fillenglen, a portion of their remaining fruit and vegetable stores, and medicine, in case the bitter cold left Belza sick. The packs had felt heavy the first several times Cylos carried them, requiring frequent stops. But he'd grown accustomed to the weight over time. With winter upon him, he was glad he'd had the summer and fall to build his strength.

In exchange, Cylos expected Belza would provide split wood from the forested taiga that was far better for fires than the scrub brush of the tundra surrounding Fillenglen, caribou meat, and, if he'd finally finished the forge he'd been working on, new weapons for the Phetos family.

Cylos yearned for the calm and peaceful Fillenglen of old he'd heard so much about from his father. Long before Cylos was born, it had once been such a haven the people barely had any need for weapons. That was when shadow casters, masters of the arcane, capable of summoning shadow creatures as powerful allies and shadow weapons as formidable arms, were still widespread throughout the land of Malgar. Although they were only a small minority of the overall populace, there had been enough that even the little town of Fillenglen enjoyed their constant vigilance and protection.

Now, as far as Cylos understood, they were all but extinct.

Most of the planet Tseloria's inhabitants were known as lonrelmians, those without any supernatural abilities, instead solely tied to one lone realm, the Tangible Realm. Whereas shadow casters possessed an innate ability to access and pull summons from the Shadow Realm, lonrelmians were constrained only to the natural, tangible world around them.

Cylos loved listening to his father's stories from before the Shadow Caster Purge, when the heroic shadow casters stood as beacons of justice and hope, protecting the innocent and defending Malgar from wrongdoing. He often imagined what it would be like to possess the ability himself, to tap into some unseen realm where majestic animals and powerful weapons could be called to his side at a moment's notice. Sometimes Cylos would play at being a shadow caster himself, using the light from the sun or the lamps in his home to project made-up figures on the wall in shadow with his hands, pretending fantastic creatures were at his side defending him.

But in reality, his musings and the stories of shadow casters felt like fairy tales compared to the life Cylos had grown accustomed to. Born fifteen years after casting was deemed illegal, he'd never even seen a shadow caster or their creatures, much less known what it was like to live under their vigilance and care.

Now Fillenglen was an easy target for wandering bands of thieves and evildoing filth of all kinds. The Lonrelmian Ministry patrollers were spread too thin, and many of them had turned corrupt anyway, especially this far on the outskirts of the Great Malgarian Plate. Thus far, the Phetos family had defended themselves with their old hunting weapons, chasing off intruders without any bloodshed, and nothing serious had befallen them. But Belza warned them of potential danger ahead and the need to be prepared with greater defenses.

He promised to provide it for them as a show of gratitude for their hospitality. Cylos's father was a good man, a strong and intelligent man, but he was a farmer by trade and not versed in the forging of weapons. Like so many others, especially in the once peaceful haven of Fillenglen, he'd grown so accustomed to shadow caster protection he hadn't imagined a world where his family would be in such danger. Though it had been more than twenty-five years since the start of the Purge, Cylos's father still held out hope things would one day improve.

There were whispers of change. Rumors of politicians advocating for caster reinstatement, that they knew where many of them had been hiding and were working to legalize the use of their unique abilities. But Cylos was skeptical. His father spoke of casters as if they could somehow will themselves back into existence. But he seemed more focused on their past magnificence than on finding solutions to revive their future. Perhaps his optimism was merely bravado. Or maybe it was simply too painful to accept that the better way of life he'd once known was gone.

Cylos found himself doubting any shadow casters were left, aside from perhaps a few still rotting in jail cells. He wasn't sure how any could still be around. He knew nothing but a world where they had been hunted and killed or imprisoned for exercising their power. If there were casters left, he wondered why they'd ever risk returning to selflessly serve Malgar.

Lonrelmians had betrayed casters. Cylos felt his people deserved what they'd brought upon themselves.

Pulling his scarf up over his nose, then slipping his gloves back on and wiggling his aching fingers as best he could, he continued his upward hike. He'd stopped for too long and needed to keep moving. It would soon be dark, and the cold would only worsen. Luckily, he was getting close, and he felt a wave of calm wash over him as he saw the point of a distant peak ahead suggesting he was nearly there. Yes, he was cold and uncomfortable, but he had plenty of stamina left. He could make the final ascent. He let out a deep exhale and tried to imagine how nice the fire in Belza's cabin would feel, along with a warm meal.

Crunch, crunch, crunch.

Cylos's head shot to the side as he heard footsteps in the snow coming from the woods to his right, shattering his pleasant thoughts.

He froze, his boot sinking into the deep snow as his last startled step was much firmer than his previous ginger paces. He narrowed his eyes to look through the trees in the fading twilight but saw nothing.

There were several explanations for the sound. A wolf or a bear perhaps, though he'd never spotted one in the months since he started making the traverse to Belza's. He forced himself to shake off his paranoia and the irrational tendency to jump to the worst-case scenario. Caribou were plentiful here, as were several other harmless creatures. That's probably all it was.

But even so, his gloved hand slid to the dagger strapped to his hip. Considering how much his hands throbbed with cold, he wasn't sure he could grip it, but that wouldn't stop him from trying.

For a moment he stood staring, well-aware the sound had stopped right as he'd looked toward it. He wasn't far from Belza's. Should he push on as quickly as he could and hope for the best? Or would he be better served by not letting his guard down?

The crunching footsteps picked up again, interrupting his contemplation. Now there was more than one set of feet.

Cylos's heart thumped inside his chest, the bitter cold forgotten as a surge of adrenaline coursed through his body. He took a hold of the dagger now, slowly unsheathing it but keeping it lowered.

It wasn't much longer before he detected movement matching the footsteps and his heart sank lower. He hadn't jumped to the worst-case scenario after all. He would have much preferred a wolf or bear over what he saw before him.

"Look, Geno, it's a kid. And judging by the pack he's carrying, I'm guessing he's got some good stuff on him. The boss'll be happy about this one."

CHAPTER 2

AN IDENTITY REVEALED

Before Cylos stood two middle-aged adults, a man and a woman, both bundled in tattered animal-fur parkas with large hoods pulled up over their heads. Their faces were fully exposed—Cylos couldn't comprehend how they were tolerating the cold—revealing a pair of wicked smiles. The broad-shouldered woman who had spoken had a quiver of arrows on one shoulder and a bow on the other. Strands of snarled black hair protruding from her hood waved in the wind as she glared at Cylos with a toothy sneer.

The bearded man with a crooked nose held a spear in one hand that looked like it doubled for a walking stick, but he lifted it and gripped it in two hands, the point directed at Cylos.

"Now what's a little boy like you doing all alone out here? You must be freezing to death. How about you come back to camp with us and we can warm you up by the fire?"

A lump formed in Cylos's throat. Despite feeling petrified, he managed to shake it off and think on his feet.

"I'm not alone. My father is just up the hill from me," Cylos bluffed. "All I have to do is shout and he'll come running. Don't lay a finger on me or you'll regret it. You're no match for him."

The man chuckled with a sneer. "Nice try. You're a clever little one,

I'll give you that. But pickings are slim out here, so we want whatever you're carrying. Yell all you want, you'll never get away from us."

His words were probably true, but that didn't mean Cylos would give up. He'd be lighter on his feet in the snow than these two, and Belza's house wasn't too far. Perhaps he could make it.

Yanking his sunken foot out of the snow, he turned and ran, weaving into the trees opposite from where the two others had emerged. "Help!" he shouted at the top of his lungs. He didn't expect Belza to hear him; he wasn't *that* close. But perhaps by yelling he could continue his bluff and the two thieves would think twice before attacking him in case he'd spoken true and had reinforcements up the hill.

Either they didn't believe him, or they didn't care, because their plodding footsteps trudging through the snow followed right behind him. Chancing a glance over his shoulder, he saw the woman nock an arrow to her bowstring.

"Oh no, not good," Cylos muttered to himself, then he cut to the right as sharply as he could as an arrow zipped past him and stuck into a tree trunk with a thud.

Running through the snow was a slogging effort. The faster he tried to go, the more he sank and struggled to get one foot in front of the other. He thought he could stay above the surface, but attempted speed eliminated his light-footedness, and he wasn't achieving the distance from his pursuers he had hoped for. Looking back again, he saw the man with the spear keeping pace, whereas the woman had stopped running, instead focusing on firing clean shots. Cylos had no idea how long he could evade her and hoped desperately she was a poor aim as she released another arrow.

He cut to his left through the thick trees and let out a second shout for help, though he realized by this point his two pursuers must have recognized his claims of a father up the hill had been a lie. Cylos continued trudging forward, surprised at how quickly evening had fallen. It was getting difficult to see, and he worried if he weaved too far into the trees, he'd lose his way and never find Belza's cabin. That was a sure way to freeze to death, assuming his pursuers didn't finish him first.

Another arrow whizzed by, but it seemed further than the first two. Maybe he would outrun them after all. He chanced one more glance over his shoulder to find the man with the spear struggling to run in the deep snow as well. He was falling behind! There was hope. Cylos just had to push on.

But right as his optimism surged, he stumbled. Stepping too close to a large pine tree, the snow beneath him gave way. He gasped as he lost his footing completely, sinking into a tree well. The rush of freezing cold took his breath away as snow entered beneath his jacket and down his waist as he suddenly found himself on his back covered in caved-in snow. Only his head, hands, and the tips of his boots protruded through the surface. He exerted all his strength to scramble up and out of the tree well, but it was no use. He'd sunk too far in the heavy snow. He was trapped.

Despite the frigid temperatures, he felt sticky sweat drip down his face and chest from the exertion of running and struggling beneath the weighty snow. He breathed heavily, desperately, beginning to accept there was nothing more he could do. He tried reaching under the snow to grab his dagger, but it was out of reach. The snow had become too packed and he couldn't maneuver in it. There was no escape.

He stopped his struggling when he heard two crunching footsteps and a chuckle. "Guess your *dad* didn't hear you. What a shame you didn't watch your step," the bearded man said.

Cylos leaned his head backward, looking at the man upside down to see a sinister grin. Cylos was terrified, but he wasn't about to give the crooked-nosed thief the satisfaction of seeing it. He gazed at him with bitter contempt, looking straight in his eyes.

The man stared back at him, the smile widening as he drew his spear back, ready to strike at Cylos.

This was it. This was the end. He was going to die here stuck in the snow. All Cylos could think was hopefully he was buried too deep so the man couldn't get the satisfaction of recovering the supplies he carried. Perhaps justice could at least be served in that small way.

But then the thief's head snapped up. Cylos's eyebrows pinched together as he watched the bearded man's triumphant sneer dissolve into wide eyes and a gaping jaw. Cylos had been so distracted by his presumed inevitable fate that he hadn't noticed the new arriving pair of footsteps until then.

The ruffian repositioned his spear, holding it up defensively, but the effort proved futile. The newcomer struck the man with a hefty mace that shattered the spear into splinters then struck the bandit square in the chest, lifting him off the ground and sending him toppling backward in a lifeless slump.

"Belza!" Cylos could hear the joy and relief in his own voice as realization dawned on him and he called his rescuer by name. To say Belza was a large man would have been a drastic understatement. He was enormous, in both height and brawn. Cylos had long felt if Belza were hitched to a wagon, he could very well outpull the family ox. His wide shoulders and rippling arm muscles were apparent even beneath the bulky deer hide coat he wore. He looked a menacing sight with his mace in one hand and a lit torch in the other. Cylos knew Belza to be mild-mannered, but he'd always suspected the massive hulk of a man was a force to be reckoned with. After watching him pulverize the thief with a single one-handed swing of his mace, no doubt remained.

The foe defeated, Belza turned to Cylos, his long white beard swaying in the wind. Belza walked forward delicately; it would be disastrous if the large man fell into the tree well himself. Then he planted his mace and torch into the snow, squatted down, and with one mighty heave, the colossal man scooped Cylos up, his arms hooking underneath the boy's shoulders to tow him out. He plopped Cylos down on his feet, safely on solid snow.

Cylos was about to thank Belza for saving his life when he remembered something much more important.

"There was another one, an archer—" The warning came a moment too late as an arrow found its mark. Cylos watched in horror as the point pierced through Belza's right upper back sticking out of his chest, the arrowhead appearing right in front of Cylos.

"No!" Cylos yelled, but his exclamation was a whisper compared to Belza's bellow of rage.

Unfazed by the attack, Belza whipped around, took a few dozen paces forward as he detached a throwing hatchet from his side, then let it fly with a mighty heave. A woman's scream seconds later was all the confirmation Cylos needed that Belza's attack had achieved its purpose.

Cylos stood still a moment in shock, but he was snapped back to reality when Belza dropped to one knee, a hand going to his injured chest where the arrow remained. The boy ran toward his rescuer and dropped to his side.

"Belza, are you alright? We've got to get back to your house, then we can start working on your wound." But as he spoke, Cylos could tell it was much worse than he'd supposed. Blood had already soaked through Belza's coat on his back and chest around the puncture, forming a crimson puddle as it dripped onto the snow below him.

"There's not enough time," Belza said in his gruff tone, stating what Cylos had already come to realize.

Cylos felt panic rise in his chest. "Not enough time? But you can't... you can't..." He forced himself to change his negative thinking. "Then, what are we going to do? Isn't there something I can do to help?"

Belza didn't mince words. "There's only one option. Bring me my torch." He used his head to motion slightly behind him where he'd left the torch planted in the snow, still burning.

Cylos's eyes widened but he didn't argue. He dashed to the torch and pulled it out of the snow. His head was spinning now. He'd heard of people burning their wounds to halt bleeding, but he wasn't sure he trusted himself to do it. At the same time, he didn't want Belza to do it to himself considering the awkward angle required to hold the torch to reach his back.

Cylos closed his eyes and tried to breathe. Maybe he was jumping to negative conclusions again. For all he knew, Belza had some other plan in mind. Perhaps he only needed the greater light the torch would provide. It had to be a possibility.

His thoughts were interrupted when he heard a snapping sound, followed by an angry pained groan from Belza. Cylos looked up to see the old man had broken off the point of the arrow. He then broke off the back with the feathered fletching as well, letting out a second grunt. Cylos had to fight off the wooziness hitting him like an avalanche at the unfamiliar gruesome sight. If he felt sick watching Belza break the arrow, he couldn't imagine what it would be like to watch him cauterize the wound.

Or worse, to do it himself.

He forced his mind into silence as he walked in front of Belza.

"Here, Belza. The torch." Cylos had to force his next words out. "What should I do with it?" He bit the inside of his cheek hard, steeling himself to heed whatever Belza asked of him, whatever was necessary to save his elderly friend, no matter how daunting.

"Take a couple steps back, and plant the torch in the snow," Belza replied. Cylos's confusion was drowned out by relief. The old man must have just needed the extra light after all. Cylos let out as subtle an exhale as he could then backed up two paces as instructed.

"A tad further," Belza directed with surprising calmness as Cylos took another half-step back. "There," Belza concluded. Cylos froze in place then stuck the bottom end of the burning torch in the snow.

"Great, now what next?" Cylos asked, hearing the positivity return to his voice upon learning he wouldn't have to perform the unthinkable.

Belza leaned his head slightly forward and stared straight into Cylos's eyes with the most serious gaze he'd ever seen from him. The old man had to be in excruciating pain and must have known time was of the essence as the wound continued bleeding, but somehow he remained calm and composed as he spoke. "I'll take care of everything from here, Cylos. But you must promise me no matter what you see, you'll keep quiet. There may be more bandits around and the last thing I want is to alert them with more noise than we've already made. Don't be startled, promise?"

Belza's hand returned to the arrow shaft protruding from his shoulder and the sick feeling returned to Cylos. Given Belza's hand placement, Cylos had a hunch about what the old man intended to do and why he'd told Cylos to keep quiet. He had half a mind to ask Belza why he needed the torch in such a specific spot just to pull the arrow out. Or if he'd need help bandaging it after. Or how he intended to halt the bleeding before they arrived back at his cabin. But, trusting Belza and knowing there was no time to lose, he simply nodded, murmuring, "I promise."

Belza gave a subtle nod in return, then proceeded as Cylos had expected. Forming a fist around what remained of the broken arrow shaft, he let out a sharp exhale then jerked. Cylos slammed his eyes shut, unsure why he hadn't turned away to begin with, and bit his tongue to prevent a sound escaping as he fought back nausea rising in his gut and throat. Belza gave out a louder groan than when he'd broken the arrow but still reacted far calmer than Cylos could have thought possible.

A few heartbeats that felt like an eternity passed and Cylos finally mustered the courage to open his eyes again. The worst had to be over at this point, although he still had no idea what Belza intended to do next. Despite realizing there would likely be a gory scene before him, curiosity got the better of him as he looked to see how the old man would care for himself.

Cylos's eyes were immediately drawn to the increased blood flow from the wound and the growing mass of red on the snow below Belza, and he regretted opening his eyes in the first place. But his disgust was replaced with confusion as his gaze lowered to settle on Belza's hands.

The old man held both extended into the torchlight before him. His pointer and middle finger on his right hand were separated, crossing the same fingers on his left. His ring fingers were bent halfway down while his pinkies pointed straight up and his thumbs straight down.

What was Belza doing? Cylos was close to breaking the silence to ask him, when he looked up at Belza's face and saw his eyes intently focused on his own hands. Cylos didn't dare break Belza's concentration. Whatever he was up to, it wasn't random or distracted. Belza's actions were intentional, though as blood continued coursing from his upper chest, Cylos found them not only strange but futile.

Another couple heartbeats passed. Cylos opened his mouth but was again rendered speechless as movement caught his eye. He had been so focused on Belza's wound and hands he'd never considered looking at the projected shadow on the snow-covered ground formed by the light from the torch and the odd shape of Belza's fingers. From out of the shadow, black misty tendrils began swirling. A pit formed in Cylos's stomach. What was happening?

He'd barely had time to process that Belza was the one to create the shadowy reaction when a lifeform materialized out of the shadowed projection where the wisps of moving shadow had first appeared. Where nothing but snow and the shadow of Belza's hands had been moments before now stood a squatty little creature on its hind legs with stubby arms, short bristly fur, and a long hollow snout sticking straight off its face.

It let out a small sound like a chirp mixed with a squeak, then waddled forward as if uncomfortable so close to the heat of the torch. Its discontent immediately ceased when it detected the blood dripping from Belza's shoulder. The old man lowered his left hand and the odd creature jumped in Belza's palm, then scurried up his arm to rest on top of his right shoulder above the wound.

As it leaned its face close to where the arrow had been removed, a silver-gray tongue protruded from its snout. Repositioning itself to find its way through the puncture in Belza's clothes, it began licking the wound, allowing Cylos a better look at it. The pointed ears and large dark eyes made it even more distinct than the previous features the boy had noticed. But what stood out most was its chest where a symbol of spiraling triangles—slender and defined at the center, wider and fading at the exterior—was visible.

Cylos would recognize that mark anywhere. His father had described it to him countless times in his stories from before the Purge. It eliminated any miniscule traces of uncertainty Cylos had about what he'd witnessed.

Belza was a shadow caster.

CHAPTER 3

THE CABIN

Cylos now understood Belza's plea for silence and composure no matter what happened, because the sight of the shadow creature summoned into existence by the old man had left Cylos's mind spinning. From the fall into the tree well and near death at the hands of the thief, to Belza's surprise rescue and the shocking revelation of his hidden ability, it was all dizzying. It took every bit of restraint Cylos had to resist shouting questions at the hermit who'd kept his true identity hidden from him all this time.

Instead, after watching the odd tube-snouted creature move from Belza's chest to his back and realizing the bleeding was rapidly decreasing, Cylos at least managed to keep his voice down as he stammered, "Belza, y-y-you're a... you're a..."

The old man nodded and his face remained emotionless. "Yes. We'll talk about it later. We still need to get to the cabin right away in case there are more brigands around."

Cylos nodded back, then, coming to his senses, spoke more easily but still barely above a whisper. "But the arrow. The wound. It looked awful. Are you sure you'll be alright?"

A proud smile touched the corners of Belza's lips. He inclined his head toward the creature perched on his broad shoulder. "This here is called a panghordra. It's a special shadow creature possessing saliva capable of healing wounds. I'll recover much faster than I would with lonrelmian means of treatment. Besides, with the bleeding stopped, a sore back won't impede me from walking. Let me give the little critter a moment longer, then we'll be on our way."

Of course Belza was undeterred. Not only was he as big as an ox, he was as tough as one. From Cylos's first time meeting the old hermit, he'd considered him unbreakable. He wondered if Belza hadn't been able to summon the shadow creature, if perhaps he still would have found a way through. Then again, Cylos had picked up a hint of desperation when Belza asked him to retrieve the torch, as if he'd only revealed his power because he saw no alternative. So maybe now the old man was downplaying the severity of the situation.

The endless questions bouncing around Cylos's head would have to wait. Belza whispered, "Dissipate," to the panghordra, and Cylos watched in wonder as the shadow spiral beneath its neck illuminated before the squatty creature disappeared in a swirling tangle of shadowy tendrils.

"Now let's get a move on. Stay close," Belza said gruffly, lifting the torch out of the snow. Cylos nodded, striving to display determination in his stoic frown, then cinched up the straps on his pack to show he was ready to go. Belza began tramping through the snow, surprisingly light-footed for a man of his stature, and Cylos kept up easily, using the packed snow imprints from Belza's footsteps to avoid sinking and keep a good pace.

Cylos was glad for Belza's presence because without it he was sure he would have gotten lost after his detour in the woods in the fading twilight transitioning to nightfall. But after less than twenty minutes of hiking, Cylos saw the silhouette of Belza's cabin sheltered in the trees ahead. He'd been so close.

Reaching the entrance, Belza pulled out a keyring with three large golden keys, each one opening a separate lock on his home's front door. After unlocking it, he opened the door and ushered Cylos inside. Cylos had forgotten how cold it was outside until warmth from the fire in the hearth filled his soul as if thawing him out down to his very bones. He allowed himself to exhale deeply and unslung his pack from his shoulder, setting it on Belza's round wooden table in the center of the single-roomed cabin as he'd always been instructed.

Normally, he would empty the supplies and show Belza everything he brought. But after all they'd experienced, once Belza shut the door behind him, Cylos couldn't hold the questions in any longer.

"Belza, how did you find me? Did you hear me call for help? And who were those thieves? What did they want with me? And... and... shadow casting? All this time you... you... you're a shadow caster?" The words poured unabated from Cylos's mouth, the final two hanging in the air as if the title alone carried mysticism and hopefulness.

Belza chuckled. "Easy now, my boy, one question at a time. I wasn't sure if you'd come today. Wouldn't have blamed you; it's brutal out there. Though I do appreciate it, I needed the supplies. When it started getting late, I thought it best to keep an eye out for you just in case. I *did* hear you shout, but wouldn't have if I hadn't been out, so you're lucky I followed my intuition."

"I'll say," Cylos said. Then he jerked his head up and felt his eyes widen as realization struck him. "How rotten of me. I never even said thank you. I... Well... You..." Cylos had to fight back tears recalling the moment the spearman was poised to strike. Cylos's adrenaline was long gone and the raw feelings of fear now felt more vivid.

His voice cracked as he said, "You saved my life, Belza. Thank you so much."

Belza stepped forward and rested a hand on Cylos's shoulder. The hermit's massive palm felt heavier than his pack had, but Cylos recognized this as Belza's form of giving comfort.

"There's no need to mention it. I know you're grateful. A lot happened at once. You have nothing to feel bad about."

"Thank you," Cylos murmured, allowing his momentary guilt to evaporate.

"Now, regarding your other questions." As Belza began to speak, he removed his hand from Cylos and gingerly peeled off his deer hide coat, using tenderness and caution around his wound. Cylos approached him and took hold of one of the sleeves, helping him.

"Thank you, dear boy," Belza said. "I have no idea who those thugs were and I can only imagine it was merely misfortune on your part that they harassed you. But I can't say I'm surprised they've moved in. There are many places to hide in the forest and Fillenglen is an exposed target. They're probably setting up a camp in the mountains where they can organize raids of your village and then escape undetected. We'll have to warn your parents and the townsfolk."

Cylos nodded acknowledgment, but Belza's pursed lips and the way his final phrase hung in the air suggested there was something more on his mind. The man remained in silence a moment before adding, "Or perhaps... they've come here looking for me."

Cylos gasped. "Why would they be looking for you?" No sooner had the words left his mouth than the boy felt foolish for asking, a feeling worsened by Belza tilting his head to the side and raising an eyebrow, but then Cylos clarified himself. "What I mean is, how would they know you were... well... worth looking for?"

Belza's skeptical expression softened and he nodded a couple times, removing his fur hat to reveal thinning white hair sitting in a messy tangle atop his head. "A good question. I can't say for sure, but speculation can cause rumors. Rumors can spread quickly. And they can spark curiosity. And regardless of if they're true or not, rumors can coerce desperate people into pursuing them. A hermit like me living alone in the mountains... In today's world, that's enough of a potential clue for anyone to suppose I might be a shadow caster."

This comment left Cylos eager to ask more, but he refrained, not wishing to interrupt.

"Tell me, Cylos. Were you frightened to see me shadow cast? Do you think worse of me now knowing what I am?"

Cylos's jaw dropped. "Worse of you? Of course not, Belza. My father adored shadow casters. He's told me so much about them. It's always been my dream to meet one. I'll admit it surprised me... maybe startled me a little. But not because I was scared of you or what you were doing. It was just all so... new to me. I didn't really know what I was seeing or what to expect, you know?"

"I understand, Cylos. And I'm glad to hear it," Belza replied. "Your father is a good man. A wise man. Much of what lonrelmians have invented about shadow casters is pure lies. While there were some who strayed from the correct path, those of us who keep to our traditional mantles and uphold the sacred pledge we swore to, we are the last ones you should ever fear, no matter what current laws suggest."

Cylos thought of all the time he'd spent alone with Belza in his cabin following deliveries. How warmly he'd always received him. His genuine conversations and jokes. The way his lessons helped the boy feel confident and capable.

He thought of how Belza had stepped directly in harm's way to save his life.

"I don't care what the law says. I would never fear you, Belza. I trust you as much as anyone."

Belza's smile increased and he stepped forward to ruffle the hair on Cylos's head. "You're a good lad, Cylos. You and your family give me hope for lonrelmians, and for the future of casters as well."

A realization struck Cylos. "Wait... do my parents know—" Belza nodded before he could finish, causing Cylos's jaw to drop again. Cylos stood in silence a moment, then his eyes narrowed and he opened his mouth to speak, but Belza cut him off.

"They felt it best to keep it a secret until you were ready, and I respected their wishes," he said, as if reading his mind. "They also wanted to keep you safe. Knowledge can be dangerous when the wrong people come asking questions. But the arrow wound was quite serious. I had no choice but to summon my panghordra to heal me, so now you know. I'll explain it to them."

"But how did *they* find out? Or why did you feel safe telling them? There's so much I want to know," Cylos pleaded.

Belza sighed. "There's no reason to keep it from you now. I've had to relocate several times over the years, Cylos. I came to Fillenglen to find a new place to live, to hide. When your father introduced himself, he wasn't shy about sharing his thoughts on shadow casters and the current state of Malgar and the Ministry."

Cylos fought a smile as he rolled his eyes. That sounded like his dad alright.

"Frankly," Belza continued, "he'd do well to use more caution. Some Malgarians can get away with outspokenness. Your father's not nearly prominent enough, if you know what I mean. He'd be wise to avoid drawing attention to himself from the wrong kind of people. Luckily for him, I appreciated his response and could detect his sincerity. I suppose it was risky for me as well, but I like to think I'm a great judge of character, so I told him what I truly was and why I'd come."

"You know, Belza, I think my father's wiser than you think. He knows when and who to share his true thoughts with. He was probably so direct with you because he suspected what you were from the beginning. He only needed you to confirm it."

Belza tilted his head and pursed his lips. "Hmm... fair point. I suppose I hadn't considered that. Regardless, as soon as he knew, he understood why I wasn't planning to stay in the village. He promised to help me remain hidden and deemed it best you be the one to bring me supplies. Said it would raise less suspicion among nosy neighbors if he assigned it as a menial chore to his son for trading rather than take it on as a priority himself. I take it your treks have gone unnoticed?"

Now it was Cylos's turn to consider. He'd found it odd his father had asked him to make the dangerous trek alone but he'd been so worried about letting him down he'd accepted without question.

Belza's explanation made sense. Of course there had been a larger reason behind his assignment.

Maybe his father would have shared more with him rather than hiding it if Cylos had been brave enough to ask.

"I suppose you're right," Cylos answered. "No one asks my parents where I am and probably don't realize when I'm gone. If they do, they'd never guess I've been trekking up and down the mountain. But they'd notice if Dad was gone that often and wonder what he was up to."

Belza nodded. "There you have it. But I'm afraid your attackers are a bad sign. Whether they impose a threat on Fillenglen or on me, I won't stand by and do nothing."

Cylos's shoulders tightened. "What are we going to do?"

"Tonight, we'll get some rest. You need it and my wound certainly needs it. Then I'll take the return trip with you in the morning. We'll warn your family of the potential threat. If your father sees fit, he can spread the word throughout Fillenglen. I'll keep hidden, but I'll be ready to help if I'm worried your family or others could be in danger."

"By help, do you mean... casting?"

Belza's gaze hardened as he stared into space. Cylos got the distinct impression Belza was replaying vivid thoughts or memories in his head. What those were, Cylos would never venture to ask.

"Only if I must. I've become well-versed in Tangible Realm weapons as well, if you hadn't noticed. But I won't let Lonrelmian Ministry law or my own safety get in the way of the Shadow Caster Pledge I've sworn an oath to uphold. If saving innocent lives is at stake, I'll cast if I must."

Cylos's eyebrows shot up. "Couldn't that get you in trouble?"

The old man shot him a mischievous grin. "Why do you think I've had to relocate so many times? And to more remote places each time..." His grin dropped into a grimace. "I fear it's only a matter of time until my description is known across Malgar. I'm not exactly inconspicuous," he said, stretching out his large arms. "That's when I'll be in real trouble. The last town I lived in, well, things didn't exactly end well."

"Where was that?" Cylos asked.

"Sentinalia," Belza replied. "Do you know where it is?"

"I've heard of it, but I don't know much about it."

Belza looked at the boy with longing eyes. "It's a beautiful town. In many ways, I wish I could have stayed there the rest of my life, lived there in peace. Sentinalia unfortunately has corrupt people in positions of power hampering the town and making it dangerous for casters, but in general the people are wonderful. I believe it could be one of Malgar's thriving towns if the right changes were enacted. You should visit someday. I'd very much like to return... but I don't think that's possible now."

Something about the way Belza described the town struck Cylos. Belza's admiration for it was clear, and if he saw so much in it, Cylos hoped he could visit one day as well. "Is that why you think the thieves who attacked me might have been part of a group pursuing you? Do you think someone from Sentinalia shared your description with them?" Cylos wondered if perhaps he could get a story out of the old man.

Belza shrugged. "It's possible," he said, his tone dry. "But whether they seek me specifically or are merely out looking for anyone in hiding they suspect could be a caster, I couldn't say for sure."

Apparently Cylos would have no such luck. He continued with his questions anyway.

"But what could they want from you? What do they get out of it? What's the point of trying to find more shadow casters? You're all mostly gone as it is, right?"

This time, Cylos was certain he saw pain in Belza's vacant stare. "We are. I've lost so many who were dear to me..." Belza fell silent and Cylos was worried he'd said too much.

But Belza moved off the subject, addressing Cylos's other questions instead. "There are still those who reward handsomely for the elimination of casters. These bandits could be bounty hunters, looking to rake in a fortune if someone wants more casters dead. Or, perhaps me specifically.

"Or maybe it's not a question of money at all. You forget the Purge started when lonrelmians collectively decided they didn't want casters around anymore. They didn't trust us, they feared us. For some anti-casters, whose conviction and hatred run deep, hunting us down and killing us is reward enough. To them, only the total extermination of casters will suffice."

A shiver ran down Cylos's spine at the thought. "But no one knows how a baby is or isn't born with casting, right? I thought Father told me it's not always genetic. For all we know it could never go away, right?"

Belza nodded. "True, but suppose someone learns they can cast, why would they do it in these conditions where they'd be locked up or worse? If a child discovered they had the ability, they'd be forced to hide it. And while the ability to cast is inherent, mastery is learned. With none to teach or guide, and no consistent way to practice and grow, casters could hardly expect to learn to adequately defend themselves or train their creatures. I'm afraid unless casting is somehow made legal again, our craft will be all but erased. When the survivors like me are gone, I don't know how shadow casting will continue."

Cylos let his gaze drop to the ground as he lowered his head. "I'm so sorry, Belza. For all of it." He wished there was something he could do. Wished he could change the world for Belza and others like him. But he was tiny, helpless, insignificant.

He let a moment of heavy silence hang in the air, hesitating to ask what he wanted to next. When Belza did nothing to break it, Cylos finally gave in.

"Belza. Even if casting were made legal again, why would you ever want to come back to serve and protect lonrelmians? After all we've done to you, why would you ever help *us*?"

Cylos was surprised by Belza's heavy exhale. The giant of a man stepped forward and dropped to one knee, putting a hand on the boy's shoulder again. His wrinkled forehead and powerful eyes showed no anger or frustration, but Cylos could tell he was serious about what he had to say.

"Tell me, Cylos. What have *you* ever done to me? To other casters?"

"What do you mean?"

"You said, after all *we've* done. You included yourself in that, so I wanted to know what you have done."

Cylos understood now. "I meant *we* as in lonrelmians. People like me."

"I know what you meant, but it's not what I asked. What have *you* done, Cylos?"

Cylos's surprise and confusion had returned. He gave the only true answer he could think of and hoped it was what Belza was looking for. "Well, nothing, I suppose."

The corners of Belza's lips perked up. "Exactly. Don't blame yourself for the actions of others, Cylos. There are countless lonrelmians like you and your family across Malgar. Good, honest people of integrity. People who want casting back nearly as much as casters themselves do.

"You should never judge the character of many by the actions of one, Cylos. Why would casters come back to serve and defend lonrelmians, you ask? Because true shadow casters don't serve types of people, we serve justice, peace, balance, and harmony. We seek to defend good in all its forms and eliminate evil in all its forms. The times and circumstances we live in are tragic. But I would never hold a preconceived grudge against all lonrelmians for the travesties of some."

Belza paused for a moment, then let out a sigh before speaking with his eyes closed. "If only the lonrelmians who pushed for a purge had viewed casters the same way. Blaming the guilty individuals rather than incriminating the entire collective. If those lonrelmians had understood the lesson I'm trying to teach you now, Malgar's entire fate and likely its destiny would have been much different. Countless lives would have been spared on both sides."

Another silence ensued and Cylos was grateful Belza allowed him time to think. Nearly his whole life, he'd blamed his fellow lonrelmians —himself, really—for what had gone wrong in Malgar, for the expulsion of casters, former vanguards of harmony. He'd always been ashamed to be lonrelmian, for being part of the problem.

For the first time, he saw things differently.

"There's still one problem, Belza," Cylos began, sticking out his chin.

The hermit cocked an eyebrow. "Oh?"

"You're right, I have done nothing wrong to casters. But that's not enough. I don't want to just say I've done nothing. I want to actually *do* something. I want to help. To be a force for good. I want to influence change. If none of us should be judged for our collective selves, then I want to become an individual who made a difference. A lonrelmian who stood up for what's right. Who stood up for casters."

Cylos felt like he'd grown half a meter taller as he puffed out his chest and spoke with pride. Belza remaining down on one knee probably helped the illusion. This wasn't like Cylos. He went along with what he was told. Played it safe. Tried to blend in and follow instructions rather than push back or stand out. His father longed for the days of casters, but he'd done little but wish for them. Cylos had felt resigned to do the same.

But the conviction and determination swirling in his chest as he locked eyes with Belza were undeniable. There was a lot Cylos didn't understand, but he knew one thing for certain. Although he couldn't be a caster himself, he too wanted to serve their cause. He wanted to be an upholder of justice, peace, balance, and harmony. And he'd do everything in his power to live the rest of his life accordingly.

Belza's grip on his shoulder increased. "You make me proud, Cylos. You've answered many of your own questions now. It's because of people like you that casters yearn to come back and serve Malgar as we did before. People like you give me hope. Hope that one day lonrelmians will stand up for what's right together, and we will be restored."

They locked eyes a moment longer, then Cylos couldn't help it. He threw himself into the old man in the largest embrace he could muster, barely able to reach around to his immense back. Belza returned the hug, his massive hands dwarfing Cylos's stature.

The moment combined with Belza's encouraging words left Cylos wishing to speak of happier, more hopeful topics, anticipating a restful and uplifting evening. As they broke the embrace, Cylos was about to ask Belza if he truly thought casters could be reinstated and what he knew about discussions and advancements in the Lonrelmian Ministry. Maybe Belza would even show him more shadow casting.

But the instant Cylos opened his mouth, Belza held up an open palm to silence him, his face stern. The old man tiptoed to a side wall of the cabin, listening intently.

It took mere seconds for Cylos to detect what had caught his attention—the crunching sound of footsteps on snow.

And by the sound of it, there were a lot of them.

CHAPTER 4

LEVIAKHUS

Cylos's heart pounded in his chest. He didn't know how much more of this he could take. Peeking through a gap in the wood, Belza moved subtly as if probing the scene outside, then he looked at Cylos with a finger to his lips. The boy remained rooted in place as the footsteps drew nearer.

Then they stopped all at once. Cylos imagined someone had called a halt.

"Listen up!" a voice shouted from outside. The tone was deep but raspy. It reminded Cylos of someone who needed to clear their throat. The man continued. "We know you're in there. You can come out peacefully, or we can burn you out. Your choice."

Cylos looked at Belza in eager anticipation.

The hermit closed his eyes and exhaled. "I'm on my way. I need only put on my coat." Belza's booming voice came across much stronger than that of the man who'd extended the threat.

"You have thirty seconds," the raspy voice answered.

"That's more than sufficient," Belza called, a tinge of annoyance coming through this time.

Cylos's eyes grew wide. Belza was going to leave the safety of the cabin?

"Belza, what are you—"

"Shh," he interrupted, then pointed across the room. "Go to my trunk and bring me the brown cloth on the top right. Hurry."

Despite his head spinning with confusion, Cylos didn't argue. As Belza slipped back into his bulky deer hide coat, grimacing as he pulled it over the still-recovering wound below his shoulder, Cylos moved as quickly but light-footedly as he could toward the trunk. Opening it up, he saw the brown cloth right away, wrapped around something round. Grabbing the bundle, he turned and dashed back to hand it to Belza.

"Thank you," the old man said, pulling something out of the cloth Cylos couldn't distinguish, then tucking it beneath his coat on the left side. Cylos heard two clicks and the sound of a strap tightening as Belza's hands worked against his chest, but the boy couldn't see past the front of the coat to know what Belza was doing.

"This is a good sign," he whispered to Cylos. "If scum like this already knew I was a caster, they wouldn't dare give me time to face them, they'd just attack. Maybe I can talk sense into them yet to avoid a conflict."

"Hurry up!" the raspy voice called again from outside. "I'm losing my patience."

"I'm coming!" Belza roared back over his shoulder. Then he looked straight at Cylos, his eyes narrow. "Stay right here and keep quiet. If anything happens to me or you hear me shout, 'That is all,' then head to the trapdoor in the floor right behind my trunk. Get inside and don't leave until morning. Understand?"

Cylos *didn't* understand. But Belza's frown and urgent tone left him feeling optionless. How could he argue? He simply nodded, his head bouncing up and down as fast as his racing heart.

Belza nodded in return then stomped to the door. Cylos noticed the brown cloth he'd given to the old man drop to the floor.

"But your shoulder?" Cylos managed to get out.

"I'll be fine," Belza grumbled without looking back at the boy, speaking in a tone Cylos couldn't fathom disputing with.

The hermit pushed his door open hard, letting it swing wide and crash into the exterior side of the wall. "What's the meaning of this?" he bellowed. Then he stepped out and let the door shut behind him.

A part of Cylos felt petrified, rooted to the spot where he stood. But another part of him burned with curiosity. What was Belza about to do?

Cylos stood still for but a moment. Remembering the old man's wry comment about how many times he'd relocated, the latter of Cylos's conflicted feelings won out. He creeped to the side of the cabin, finding the largest gap between logs he could, to peer out and take in the scene as best as possible.

A man with shoulder-length hair sticking out from a hood and fur hat stood a few paces ahead of eight others who were arranged in a curve behind him about two meters apart. Some bore torches while others held glowing light-rods, a less common but more reliable light-producing device, to illuminate their way. A grin spread across Cylos's face as the bandit in the front was forced to tilt his head upward, even from the distance, to size up the massive man they'd disturbed.

With wide eyes and a shaky chin, the long-haired man initially looked as though Belza's stature might cause him to wilt under his gaze. But the surprise soon transformed into a sneer. Regaining his poise, he snarled at Belza, "We found two of our comrades dead in the woods. And followed your trail here. We're here to make sure you pay for what you did."

If Belza was intimidated while outnumbered nine to one—perhaps more if there were others Cylos couldn't see—he sure didn't show it. "For what *I* did?" he boomed. "More like they paid for what *they* did. They're the ones who attacked me unprovoked. I'm an old hermit; I live alone here in my cabin. I only want to be left alone."

The other man chuckled. "*They* attacked *you*? Geno and Muffy might not have been the smartest of the bunch, but they'd know better than to take on a brute like you by themselves. They were far too cowardly."

"I don't care about your assumptions. They were the aggressors. I did only what was necessary to defend myself. But I take no pleasure in harming anyone. So, you can learn from their mistakes and stand down to avoid a similar fate. If you go away and leave me be, we can all go on living to fight another day in these challenging times."

Cylos held his breath. Would these ruffians take his offer?

A scoff from the long-haired, raspy-voiced man answered the question. "You think *we're* the ones that need to learn and go away? Old man, we've got you outnumbered nearly ten to one and you have no element of surprise. You think we're scared of you?"

Belza ignored the question. "I have nothing of value and if you're scrounging for meaningful supplies, you'll be disappointed. These days I hardly have enough for myself. It would amount to nothing if you divvied it up amongst yourselves."

The intruder let out a wicked chuckle. "Are you hard of hearing, old man? This has nothing to do with supplies. You killed two of our comrades and we won't tolerate that. Our boss has big plans for Fillenglen. We can't let some hermit on the outskirts thinking he can get away with what you've done. Wouldn't be right to give those villagers any false hope about standing up to us. We have a reputation to keep if the people from Fillenglen are to serve us the way we plan."

Cylos barely noticed his hands had clenched into fists. These lowlifes had moved into the mountains and were going to strike against the village. His village. How dare they?

"So, you've got two options. You can throw down your weapons and come back with us in chains so we can take what we want from your little house and make an example out of you to the Fillenglen citizens, or if you refuse, we will cut you down where you stand. Oh, and in case you think we were too daft to notice, we saw the second pair of tracks. We know you've got a young one inside. Make the right choice and *maybe* we'll spare them."

Cylos's eyes shot open and he had to suppress a gasp. His hand instinctually dropped to the dagger at his side. Belza had ordered him to stay put, but how could he stand there and do nothing? Especially after what he had pledged to Belza right before these thugs showed up. No matter what happened, he didn't want to give these vile oppressors the pleasure of defeating him without a fight. But he was also terrified. Both of the threat the intruders posed and of upsetting Belza. So he decided to exercise restraint, waiting to see what Belza would do first.

If the large man was intimidated by the invader's threats, he didn't show it. In fact, his stern scowl looked more bored and unimpressed than it did worried.

A smug grin perked up on the corners of Belza's lips. "I'm afraid you're incorrect about the element of surprise and the number of options I have at my disposal," he said.

The raspy man let a smirk stretch across his face. "Oh yeah? Please, enlighten me," he bit back with sarcasm.

Belza's glare transformed as his eyebrows slanted and his eyes narrowed into a tense, rageful stare. "Gladly."

His right hand soared to the left side of his chest like lightning and after a loud *thunk*, Belza whipped his shoulders back to loosen his coat, causing it to drop down his arms to expose his chest. A bright beam of light projected from where his hand had struck moments earlier, shining down on the ground before him.

Cylos flinched in surprise, only then realizing what must have been in the brown cloth he'd retrieved for Belza. He'd heard his father tell of them in his stories. A caster beam—a distinguishing round button worn by casters on the front of their vests that was a dull gray when turned off, but produced a bright ray of light when the bulb inside was activated. It provided a constant light source for forming shadow symbols if others were unavailable.

Unfortunately, the enemies recognized it, too. "He... That's a... What?" Shrinking back, the long-haired man stumbled over his words, then shrieked, "He's a caster, kill him!"

But Belza was far too quick. The instant the light had ignited, he'd placed his arms in its beam to project a shadow. His right forearm crossed his left arm at the inside of the elbow, his right index finger, thumb, and pinky extended while on the left hand only the pinky stuck out. By the time the arrows, stones, and spears came flying toward Belza, a creature unlike anything Cylos had seen had already materialized before him.

The beast had a dark green body like a thick snake but with eight stubby, clawed legs supporting it. Though currently curled up—four of its legs on the ground, four elevated—it looked like it would extend as long as the cabin if stretched out to its full length. Pivoting on its grounded feet, it swung its head, which Cylos thought looked part-reptile, part-fish, part-monster. With its swift strike, it intercepted and dismantled each of the incoming projectiles with a combination of snapping jaws and slashing claws tangled in shadowy mist that shifted with its every movement. As it stopped the attacks, dark, finger-like tendrils coming off sharp purple crests on either side of its head whipped back and forth, while its long body swung side-to-side.

While the fear-striking creature performed its initial defense of Belza, the caster formed another symbol with his hands until a pure black crossbow appeared in his grip out of a swirl of dark mist. Holding it in both hands, Belza fired an initial shot, picking off the thief farthest to his right.

As if recognizing its master was now armed, the creature abandoned its defensive stance and plunged headfirst into the deep snow beneath it, until its full, long body had burrowed beneath the surface, disappearing from view. Shouts and gasps erupted from the onlookers, who fired at the spot in the snow where the creature had been moments before.

During their panicked retaliation, another shadowy bolt appeared on the top of Belza's crossbow, and he released another fatal shot.

Bearing a curved scimitar, the raspy-voiced superior cried out, "Aim for the caster. Kill him and the shadow creature will go away too. Don't let his monster distract—auugghhhh!"

The dark green creature's head shot out of the snow, breaking the surface right beneath the leader before he could finish his directive, sending snow spraying in all directions. The shadow creature launched him upward off his feet then caught him in its mouth in midair and tossed him aside into the woods like a ragdoll. Some of the other scoundrels shot at it, but the projectiles bounced off harmlessly and the beast submerged beneath the snow again.

Cylos was astounded by the way it disappeared under the surface by burrowing with unnatural speed. Then, after only a couple heartbeats, it popped up in similar fashion beneath another bandit, sending her flying in the air, while also shooting two of its eight clawed legs out of the snow to grab then hurl two others. Panicked screams filled the night as the shadow creature launched then grabbed Belza's adversaries before flinging them aside with either jaws or claws.

Belza only had to unleash one more bolt before his shadow creature finished the job, twice more disappearing beneath the snow then reappearing with an explosion of icy particles as it broke the surface, taking out hapless victims each time. Soon all nine were defeated, and a sudden silence, so recently filled with shouts of terror, filled the night air. It was almost eerier than the previous yelling and explosions of snow from the shadow creature.

Cylos stood gaping, unsure how to process what he'd witnessed. The panghordra had been startling because he'd never witnessed casting. This legged serpent, or whatever it was, was startling for far more indisputable reasons. From its daunting appearance to its unmatched speed, it was far more than startling to foes. It was downright terrifying. Cylos was glad Belza was on his side.

The shadow creature descended beneath the snow once more before it reemerged out of the first hole it had created to stand at Belza's side. It once again curled up so its head came right to Belza's chest. Belza tossed aside his crossbow as if it were worthless, and after a clunk on the snowy ground, it disappeared in a swirl of shadowy tendrils. He then held up an open palm as the scaly creature nuzzled its dark green head into Belza's hand, letting out a chirp and a purr.

Suddenly it looked far more friendly and docile than it had before. Cylos still found the creature terrifying, but now it looked almost peaceful as it interacted in celebration of a well-executed victory with its master.

"Cylos, get out here," Belza bellowed. Cylos's heart skipped a beat, but he didn't argue. After what he'd witnessed, he couldn't imagine ever arguing with Belza again.

He popped open the door and creeped forward, his eyes never leaving the shadow creature. It turned and looked at him with calm, wide eyes, its enormous tongue flicking out in greeting.

"Don't be alarmed, Cylos. I assume you were watching, weren't you?" Belza asked. The old man knew him too well.

Cylos could only nod in return, his throat still too tight to form words.

"Then I can understand why you'd be nervous, but don't be. This is one of my most loyal and obedient shadow creatures. It won't harm you. Come say hello."

Cylos's breath caught in his chest and the hair on the back of his neck stood straight up. He was sure he looked stupid with his jaw gaping. He wasn't sure if he was exhilarated or terrified, but somehow

Belza's calming presence reassured him it was okay. Mustering his courage, Cylos took a few steps forward, and soon the creature's head bent down to his chest level.

"Give it your palm like I did," Belza instructed.

Cylos slowly raised a trembling hand and soon felt the shadow creature's scaled skin nuzzling into his open palm, its wide nostrils opening and closing as it familiarized itself with the boy.

It didn't take long for Cylos's previous fear to melt away and for his shaking body to relax as he instead felt a connection with the creature. He cautiously brought his other hand up to the beast, gently stroking one of the purple crests on the side of its head. Its chirping purr increased in volume.

Belza grinned as well. "This is a leviakhus. It's especially adept in water, but it can burrow through any reasonably soft surface. Perfect for enemies standing on snow, wouldn't you agree?"

"I'll say," was all Cylos managed. It had decimated the opposition and yet Belza talked about its skills so casually. Was there really a time on Tseloria when creatures such as this were commonplace? Summoned and guided by wise masters like Belza?

For the first time, Cylos understood why some lonrelmians might fear them, especially those whose misdeeds put them on casters' bad sides. But feeling the creature nestle into him, sensing its respect for its master, and knowing the kind of person Belza was, it also deepened Cylos's conviction that any fear or distrust lonrelmians had was only because they didn't understand. Belza had spoken true to the gang's leader—he acted out of defense. If they hadn't threatened him—threatened to disturb the balance Belza so dearly protected—they would have never seen the violent, powerful leviakhus, only the docile, magnificent creature Cylos rested his hands upon now.

"I hate to interrupt, Cylos, but I'm afraid we must change our plans. I don't know what those treacherous villains have in mind for Fillenglen, but it can't be good. Between the two from earlier and these nine, they're down eleven troops. Who knows how far away the others are and what they might have heard. I know we both could use rest, but I fear we can't delay. We must head to Fillenglen tonight. We need to warn the village, your parents. There's no telling when those bandits will strike."

Cylos would be lying if he said he wasn't disappointed. After such an exhausting and traumatizing journey up, he'd been looking forward to sleeping in the comfortable cot in Belza's house. But he understood.

"Then we'd better get going. It's a long walk," Cylos said, sticking out his chest to mask any second thoughts, then he turned back toward the door to go retrieve his pack. He didn't notice the huge grin on Belza's face until the old hermit cleared his throat loudly, causing Cylos to turn around and look at him.

"We won't be walking, Cylos."

It only took a subtle glance from Belza to the still-exposed caster beam on the front of his left shoulder for Cylos to catch on. A surge of anticipation raced up his body.

"I'll grab a few things, then we'll get going," the old man concluded.

CHAPTER 5

FILLENGLEN

After dissipating the leviakhus, Belza passed Cylos and reentered his house, motioning for the boy to follow him inside. Walking to his trunk, he began gathering supplies Cylos couldn't make out into a pair of large sacks, then moved to the corner of his cabin behind his bed.

"I completed the forge behind the cabin," he said, "and I had enough time to make these." On top of the bed he placed two silver swords—identical save that one was shorter than the other—a battle axe, and a bow with a quiver containing at least two dozen arrows. "These should serve your family better than what you have. Here, I made this sword for you." Belza picked up the shorter silver sword and extended it toward Cylos. "See how it feels."

Cylos was exhilarated at the prospect of receiving his own weapon. Outside of his small dagger, he'd never owned one before. He took the impressive double-edged blade cautiously from Belza's hand, stepped back, and gave it a couple swings from side to side. It felt light but sturdy. The hilt fit his grip perfectly and the lines of black and gold streaking down it provided an elegant touch.

"We can practice with it later. For now, put it in this." Belza picked up a leather scabbard and handed it to Cylos. The sword slid in easily against the interior caribou fur lining, fitting snugly as the sword tip made a satisfying *clink* against a metal cap at the end. Belza wrapped the weapons intended for Cylos's parents in a brown sackcloth and gathered up the two sacks he'd packed earlier.

He then helped Cylos secure the scabbard and sword to his back and took a step back, taking in the sight. "There, you look like a warrior already."

Cylos met Belza's proud grin with one of his own.

"Very well. Let's head outside. It's time to summon our rides," Belza said with a wink.

Between the new sword and the thought of riding shadow creatures, Cylos's former tiredness was long forgotten, replaced by eager excitement. Belza hefted the sacks and weapons onto the ground outside the cabin, then he ignited his caster beam.

Cylos watched in wonder as Belza placed his hands into the light, positioning his fingers precisely. Within moments, a creature appeared out of a swirl of black and purple misty tendrils. It reminded Cylos of the caribou common to the area, only bigger. It had the body of a deer, but a much bulkier head and longer snout like a moose with a massive set of rounded antlers branching out from either side of its head. The shadow spiral mark Cylos recognized from the previous two shadow creatures was found on each antler.

"This is an alcier," Belza explained. "It will be your ride. I've trained it well. It's the calmest and smoothest of my mounts and should move well in the snow. I'll give it instructions as we go. All you have to do is hold on. We'll be moving fast, so cover your face and lean into the alcier's neck to protect from the cold. It should provide warmth and protection from the wind as we go."

Despite having animals at home, Cylos had little experience riding them. Although Belza made it sound easy, he had a million questions he wanted to ask him. But before he got the chance, Belza was already summoning his next cast, so he kept them to himself, hoping he could catch on as easily as Belza suggested.

The next creature to appear was a strange sight. The bulky animal wasn't as tall but was far wider than the alcier. It had a pair of knobby, forked horns on each side of its head, one protruding from the top of its skull, the other below its eyes. Its leathery skin was reddish-orange along its broad back and mostly black down its thick legs. As Cylos looked into its deep black eyes, he thought its head looked something like a bald bison, only larger.

As it stared back at Cylos, it scraped a three-toed, hooved foot across the snowy ground and let out a snort that caused him to jump backward.

"Easy now, easy," Belza commanded the creature, running a hand along its neck. Once the stiffness in the creature's neck eased, Belza turned toward Cylos. "Sorry about that. This is my euobiloceros. It's feistier than most of my casts, but I trust it with my life. Most casters don't use this creature as a mount, but its size suits me. It's surprisingly fast for its bulk, so it should keep pace with the alcier."

Cylos was rendered speechless by this point. He'd gone from assuming he'd never see a caster his entire life to discovering he'd known one for months and seeing four of the strangest creatures he could never have imagined up close.

After securing the two packs and the weapons to the euobiloceros, Belza clicked his tongue twice and the alcier dropped to its knees on both its front and back legs. "Climb on," he told Cylos. "Let's get a move on."

Despite the nervousness clutching his heart, Cylos was determined not to show it. He nodded with determination, then pulled his scarf up over his face, leaving only his eyes exposed. He should have been fazed by the bitter cold, but he hardly noticed with all the adrenaline rushing through his veins. He climbed onto the alcier's back, then the creature stood up with a low bellow. Cylos stroked the back of its neck, and the creature turned its head around and tapped Cylos's leg with its black nose in a gesture Cylos took as a show of reassurance.

He then watched as Belza climbed atop his euobiloceros and, though he made it look easy, Cylos couldn't miss his grimace as he pulled himself up. The boy narrowed his eyes. Belza's wound was bothering him more than he let on.

"Here we go. Hold on tight," Belza said.

Cylos needed no second bidding. He leaned forward and threw his arms around the alcier's thick neck. Though shadowy tendrils came off the creature with its every movement, Cylos was surprised at the sturdiness of its neck, and how soft its dense hide felt against the little skin he had exposed.

Those thoughts were swept away when the alcier began its graceful sprint through the snow-covered woods. A rush of cold air felt like knives to Cylos's exposed eyes, and he tightened his grip further as he was bumped up and down with every step of the antlered mount. Once he adjusted to the speed, he allowed himself the chance to breathe and dared to open his eyes. It was incredible how fast the alcier traveled, and he looked over to see the massive euobiloceros bounding right behind, keeping pace as Belza had predicted.

Belza's caster beam was ignited to light their way, though Cylos noticed it wasn't as bright as when he'd summoned the leviakhus and the shadowy crossbow. He hoped that only meant its luminosity could be adjusted.

Assuming they made it to Fillenglen without incident, Cylos would be sure to ask him. The thought crossed his mind that perhaps the noise they made while traveling would alert nearby bandits. If it did, he took solace in knowing Belza was there to protect him. And hopefully any who saw them would be deterred by the sight of the alcier and euobiloceros. Cylos tried to push down his fright and instead enjoy the satisfying moment of riding such an elegant creature.

Cylos had spent years fantasizing about shadow creature companions at his side, aiding and protecting him. What had once felt like a fairy tale was now more real than he'd ever imagined. Experiencing the breathtaking ride atop the magnificent alcier was the most alive he recalled feeling in his entire life.

Cylos was pleased to find their descent down the snowy slope went undisturbed. When they reached the edge of the forest, both creatures came to a stop. He hadn't heard Belza issue a command, but he assumed somehow, they had halted at his bidding.

"Best not to cause any alarm in case anyone sees us entering Fillenglen. There's no tree cover on the tundra. We'll walk the rest of the way," Belza said.

Cylos slid off the alcier, giving it a loving pat on the back of its neck. It responded by bowing its head and letting out a friendly grunt.

"It enjoyed your company," Belza said, managing a grin.

"And I enjoyed riding it. It's a beautiful creature, Belza. I hope to ride it again someday."

"Ah, yes it is. And I'm sure that's an arrangement we can make." They shared a brief smile before Belza's expression turned serious. "Now, let's get to the village."

After removing the packs, Belza commanded both creatures to dissipate. Like the others, their shadow spirals illuminated momentarily before they disappeared in a swirl of shadowy tendrils. Belza then pulled out some rope and lashed the two supply bags together along with the cloth holding the weapons, then hefted them all over his uninjured left shoulder.

"What did you pack?" Cylos asked.

"My share of supplies to trade with your family, and a few other things, just in case." He'd spoken with a vague finality that left Cylos feeling he shouldn't pry further.

"Can I carry anything for you?" Cylos asked, trying to keep the concern out of his voice as he thought of the old man's grimace when he boarded the euobiloceros.

"I'm fine. Let's get moving."

Cylos couldn't hold the words back any longer. "Belza... your shoulder... it's bothering you, isn't it?"

"I told you I'm fine, Cylos. I appreciate your concern, but it isn't far. Now let's go."

Cylos lowered his head, feeling embarrassed, but he didn't argue as they began plodding through the snow. As they emerged from the tree cover into the flat tundra, Cylos could make out the glow of lights from the town of Fillenglen and he was filled with a sudden eagerness to be back home. The light also reminded him of his question from before.

"Belza, is everything alright with your... it's a caster beam, right? I noticed it looked a little dimmer on our way down."

"You're very observant," the old man replied. "But, yes, everything is fine. I can change its brightness based on circumstance. I've kept mine well maintained through the years and have backup bulbs and power sources for it should I need them. It will be fine."

Cylos's curiosity was piqued again. And though he normally hesitated to express his thoughts and questions, with nothing else to do during their walk to Fillenglen, a surge of courage allowed him to seek answers.

"How does it work? Shadow casting, I mean. You used a torch before and the beam later. Was there a difference?"

"Good questions, Cylos. It's quite simple. A shadow caster can cast with any light source, be it the light of a fire, the sun, moon, anything. A caster beam is merely a tool to ensure, no matter the time of day, weather, or environment, a light can be provided. That's why all casters bear them. The torch was the best light source when I needed the pang-hordra. But it was dark when the thieves approached the cabin and I wanted my hands free to cast, so I asked you to retrieve the beam. Make sense?"

Cylos nodded. "It does. But there's something else I have to ask. Your leviakhus... it was incredible. It took out so many people while you were nowhere close to danger. And my father told me shadow creatures can't die. If they're defeated, they just disappear and recover a while then you can bring them back. If that's all true, how were shadow casters ever defeated? Couldn't you summon an unending army of creatures to protect you?"

Belza tilted his head and eyes upward and a sad smile formed on his lips. "If only we could. Shadow casters can only safely summon two shadow creatures into the Tangible Realm at a time and it's unsafe to summon more once three have been defeated and are recovering in the Shadow Realm."

"Unsafe?" Cylos interrupted. "What happens if you try to summon more?"

Belza sighed. "Let's just say, attempting to bring that many into existence at once takes a hard toll on a caster. Pulling shadow creatures from their realm into ours is a strenuous act and abusing that power, spreading oneself too thin, can carry a steep price."

Belza trailed off, and while Cylos couldn't say he fully understood, he believed he'd picked up on the consequences Belza hinted at.

"So you see," the old man continued, "because of those limitations, by sheer numbers, lonrelmians could defeat enough casts to eventually leave casters defenseless. Many of us are formidable fighters regardless, but once three shadow creatures have been defeated and forced back to the Shadow Realm to regain their strength, which takes several hours, we become much more vulnerable."

Cylos's head was spinning at this point. "I've heard about the Shadow Realm, but I don't really understand it. Is that where the creatures come from and disappear to or something? How does it all work?"

This brought a smile to Belza's face as he chuckled. "I could spend all evening talking to you about that and you'd likely still be left confused. There are many theories and speculations. What we know is those with the ability to shadow cast, though they live in the Tangible Realm—the world you and I see before us now—they somehow enjoy an innate connection with the Shadow Realm, a realm believed to surround our own though inhabited only by creatures of shadow. By forming the appropriate shadow symbols, we can pull creatures and weapons from their realm into our own. Each shadow creature is unique to its caster, animated by a portion of the caster's soul. Thus, while other casters could all summon their own alciers, euobiloceroses, panghordras, and others, they'd all be unique individual creatures, distinct from my own."

"I think I'm following. Well, at least partially. Don't really understand how the Shadow Realm exists or how your soul is shared with a creature from it."

Belza laughed heartily this time, though he quickly threw a hand to his mouth to muffle it. "If you understood all that after one explanation, my dear Cylos, you'd rival the wisest sages among casters. Most of us simply know we have the skill and how to use it without taking time to wonder or understand how it all works."

"Do *you* understand how it all works?" Cylos asked.

Belza smiled while shaking his head. "Oh, I'd say I understand quite a bit. Let's leave it at that."

Cylos wanted to ask more, but the conversation had taken them most of the way to Fillenglen.

"Let's change the subject for now. Best not to risk anyone overhearing us." Whether Belza was exercising an abundance of caution or seeking an excuse to avoid delving into the deep topic with the young lonrelmian, Cylos wasn't sure, but he didn't contest.

A few moments later, they arrived at his home, a welcome sight. Cylos rapped his knuckles across the wooden door three times. Several moments passed, but finally the door opened a crack.

"Cylos? Cylos!" came the whisper from his father. He opened the door wider, and after he rubbed the sleep out of his eyes and extended a hand to rest it on Cylos's shoulder, his gaze darted from his son over to Belza. His jaw clenched and his eyes narrowed at the sight of the large, bearded man.

"And Belza? You're not supposed to be down here. And at this hour? Has something happened?"

Belza hesitated, looking from Cylos's father to Cylos and back. "Well, Cylos and I are both alright. But if you'll let me in, I think we'd better talk."

CHAPTER 6

THE PROPOSITION

Cylos would have liked to stay up and converse with his parents and Belza, but Belza had unpacked the supplies for the Phetos family and then only just gotten to the part about rescuing Cylos from the thieves when sleep overtook the boy. He woke up before the sun the next morning to the sound of Belza snoring from where he lay sleeping on a too-small cot nearby. Cylos found himself with a blanket wrapped around him, no doubt from his mom, on the couch where he'd sat after first getting back home.

His mother and father were surely back in their own room asleep, for all was quiet. Cylos wondered how much Belza had told his parents, how much detail he'd gone into about casting, and what plans they might have made for the morning.

Cylos wasn't sure if Belza had assumed the thugs wouldn't attack that night or if perhaps he and his father had made arrangements for a town watch to keep eyes out for any attackers so Belza could get some sleep. That wouldn't surprise him. Belza needed the rest as much as anyone. Cylos crept over to him and noticed the right side of his chest and shoulder wrapped in a treated woven bandage—Cylos's mother's handiwork. Cylos was surprised by how tired he must have been to sleep through all that.

He was contemplating whether he should lay back down, start quietly preparing breakfast for Belza and his parents, or sneak outside to see if there was any evidence of the townspeople on high alert, when he detected a sound coming from the distance, drawing nearer.

At first, Cylos thought his ears were playing tricks on him, but it didn't take long to realize it was real—the sound of hoofbeats approaching, crashing through the snowy tundra.

He hated to wake Belza, but what choice did he have? The old man would want to be present for whatever was happening.

"Belza," Cylos whispered urgently. "Belza!" he repeated more harshly. The hermit's eyes shot open, and he leaned up from the cot that wasn't large enough to fit his body. The edges of his shoulders stuck off either side and his feet hung off the end.

"Someone's coming," Cylos whispered.

Rubbing the tiredness from his eyes, Belza sat the rest of the way up. "Yes, I can hear. Go get your father."

Cylos nodded, but the command turned out unnecessary.

"I'm up, Belza," came a reply from the other room, then Cylos's father stepped through the door. His brown eyes and thin lips showed no fear, only determination.

As Cylos's mother stepped out behind him, she looked the complete opposite, her head stooped as she bit her lower lip and wrung her hands together.

Knock, knock, knock. Everyone's eyes darted to the door before anyone could speak another word. Cylos watched intently as his father motioned for Belza to scoot over to one side out of view of the door, then he walked across the room to open it. The townspeople knew about Belza—at least the part about him being a hermit living in the mountains above the town—and didn't have any problem with him to Cylos's knowledge. But Cylos was sure his father didn't want to risk any suspicion since it would look odd that Belza had stayed the night with potential foes now approaching.

As soon as his father cracked the door open, a man outside said, "Matthias, it's like you said last night. They're coming. A lot of them."

Cylos recognized the familiar voice of their next-door neighbor Lorcan. Despite the panic in his tone and the concerning report, Cylos saw the tenseness in his father's shoulders soften at the sight of his friend. At the very least, the man at his door was a trustworthy guest.

His father's response was resolute. "Let's go see what they want. Tell the townspeople to stay calm. No need to jump to conclusions."

"Please be careful," Cylos's mother issued from behind, her fingers drumming against her thighs.

Cylos's father gave a half turn and shot her a subtle grin. "Aren't I always?" he jeered. Then, turning back to Lorcan, he said, "Wait there, I'll be right out."

Shutting the door, he turned to Belza, who spoke before Matthias Phetos could get a word in. "I'm coming too. You may have convinced me to stay out of sight last night while you handled things, but if there's a threat to the village, you'll need my help. I won't reveal... what I can do... unless absolutely necessary."

"I appreciate your boldness, friend," Cylos's father began, "but I've got a better idea. Let's see what comes of their arrival before we do anything rash. There's a trapdoor in my room opening to an underground tunnel leading to a stable on the edge of town. From there, you should be able to stay hidden while viewing the proceedings." He paused then looked at his son. "Cylos, you know the way. Lead Belza there now."

"Hasn't Cylos been through enough? Shouldn't we keep him out of this?" Cylos's mom protested.

Cylos was about to argue, eager to stand up for his father's plan, but the elder Phetos spoke up before he could. "Tilly," he began with a calm voice and warm eyes. "Cylos can do this. Trust him and trust me. No matter what happens, Belza and I will keep him safe."

His father had been much more tactful than he would have been. The reassurance in his dad's tone must have been enough because his mother ran a hand through her strawberry-blonde hair then nodded acceptance.

A surge of elation mixed with terror rushed through Cylos as he grabbed his new scabbard and sword then motioned for Belza to follow.

Belza attached his caster beam to the front of his left shoulder, then put on his deer hide coat to cover both the round button of the beam and the bandage Cylos's mother had fashioned on the opposite side. He armed himself with his mace and throwing hatchets, then followed behind Cylos.

As soon as they were in the back of the house, out of sight of the entrance, Cylos heard his father open the front door and begin talking indistinctly to Lorcan for a moment, before the door shut again and he was gone. Cylos looked over his shoulder one last time to throw his mom an encouraging grin, which she returned with a firm but pleasant nod, the corners of her mouth barely perking up in a forced smile, her blue eyes misty.

All the while the hoofbeats had grown louder, until Cylos could tell they were nearly at the village's edge. "Let's get going. We don't want to miss anything."

Belza nodded agreement, then, after opening the wooden door in the floor of his father's room, the two of them descended together.

It was a tight fit for Belza weaving through the narrow tunnel, but with Cylos's guidance, they made it through then up and out into the stable just in time. Peering through a gap in the planks of the wooden walls, Cylos watched as a line of about fifty horsemen came to a slow stop outside the village. Several dozen more ruffians followed behind on foot. Each man and woman on horseback looked strong and battle-tested, their fine weaponry and armor creating a far more formidable appearance than the assailants Cylos and Belza had faced the night prior.

Among the horsemen, two riders strode a little further than the rest, both men. The first man atop a brown horse looked in his early forties, with wavy red hair and intense eyes. He wore all black with two swords strapped to his back crossing one another. The other appeared around ten years younger, but his features were challenging to make out beneath the round and slightly pointed helmet he wore covering all but his eyes and mouth. A hood on his black tunic hung down his back, and his chest was protected by a silver breastplate. He sat atop a distinctive horse, its gray body sharply contrasted by its black head, legs, and tail.

Once the commotion of the approaching group died down, the younger man of the two guided his gray and black horse forward two steps and removed his helmet to reveal short brown hair buzzed almost bald. His serious face appeared permanently hardened into a scowl. Gazing intently at the crowd of Fillenglen villagers assembled across from him—Cylos could make out his father and his neighbor Lorcan among them—the intruder spoke.

"Citizens of Fillenglen. My name is Ishaan Nikanti, second-in-command to Thaddeus Ralkentin," he began, gesturing to the other rider who had advanced alongside him. "We come with a proposition for your village."

Cylos exchanged a quick glance with Belza, who looked at him with a single eyebrow raised.

The man called Ishaan continued. "I won't mince words. We set up camp in the mountains above your village because we planned to take over Fillenglen as a base of operations and because we know you have useful supplies."

He was interrupted as a disconcerted chatter arose from the assembled villagers.

"Surely, from one glance at us, you must realize a rabble of farmers like you have neither the numbers, strength, nor skill to stand up to us. Your lives are meaningless to us, and any resistance would be futile. But" —he let the word hang in the air for a moment until the chattering villagers had quieted down—"unforeseen circumstances have left us willing to compromise. Last night several of our troops were brutally slaughtered up in the mountains, but one survived to tell what happened."

Again, Cylos and Belza looked at one another, both their jaws dropped. Cylos couldn't fathom anyone surviving the leviakhus attack. Maybe one had managed to land softly enough to only be left unconscious? Or perhaps a spare had been hiding in the woods behind the group who saw what happened then escaped undetected? It hardly mattered now.

Ishaan went on. "Based on his account and the aftermath we saw in the mountains outside a lone cabin high up by the peaks, we can say with certainty they were killed by a *shadow caster*." Cylos had never heard words delivered with such venom, as if stating them alone was as painful as swallowing a knife for Ishaan.

A collective gasp rose from the Fillenglen villagers and their previous chatter rose to loud conversation. Cylos wasn't informed enough to know whether his father's views on casters fell in the majority of Fillenglen public opinion, but he was positive there were some on both sides of the issue. If Cylos's father's views were unpopular with most, he could be in big trouble. Although his relationship with Belza had remained discreet since Cylos had been the one to deliver weekly supplies to him, it was still no secret Matthias Phetos had interacted with the old hermit more than anyone.

Ishaan rubbed a palm against his forehead and looked upward as if fighting the urge to roll his eyes at the frantic, excitable villagers before continuing his dialogue. "We believe the caster has found his way here. So, our proposition is, bring the shadow caster to us and we'll leave this place behind, sparing your village the plans we had for it. Otherwise, you should know, we aren't here to bargain, so don't think for a moment you have an alternate option. With every passing hour that you fail to deliver the caster to us, one of your people will be killed, beginning with this one."

Pointing with one hand, Ishaan gestured toward a ragged woman shielding two kids behind her who couldn't be much older than Cylos. With his other hand, he signaled to one of the horsemen behind him, who moved forward and trained an arrow on the woman Ishaan had indicated.

The woman ushered her children more tightly behind her as she gave out a scream that was joined by shouts of angst and anger from others in the crowd. Among them, one stood out louder than the others.

"Now, hold on. Stand down! There's no need to kill anyone for what you want." The voice belonged to Cylos's father.

A smile perked at the corners of Ishaan's lips. He was probably glad his show of aggression was met with fear and immediate compliance. He dropped his hand slightly and the man with the bow followed suit, releasing tension on the string and lowering the weapon. Ishaan looked at Cylos's father expectantly, but before he could speak, others from the village interrupted.

"You knew the man up in the cabin better than anyone, Matthias. Why don't you handle this and leave the rest of us out of it?" an angry woman's voice chimed in.

"How dare you shelter a caster and bring him this close to our midst?" another man shouted.

Cylos's father turned toward the voice and through narrowed eyes said, "I had no idea he was a caster, if that's even who did this."

Cylos felt his eyes widen. "What's he saying?" he whispered incredulously. But Belza held a hand to his shoulder. "He's doing what he thinks is best to protect himself, you, your mother, and me. Don't mistake his bluff for cowardice."

Cylos let out a deep exhale and felt the tension escape from his body. He could understand what Belza was saying.

The man who had challenged Matthias spoke up again. "Oh, and who *else* would be up so high in the woods in this cold near that cabin? Don't play dumb with us, Phetos. You heard the man. Turn the caster in and they'll leave us alone. If anyone knows where he is, it's you. Should anyone in this village be killed by them, their blood will be on your hands. Make the right decision."

Cylos's jaw started to ache and he realized he was gritting his teeth. He didn't recognize the weasely voice of whoever was speaking to his father, but he didn't like him. He especially didn't like how eager he was to turn Belza over to this vile gang.

Ishaan's attention was now focused on Cylos's father. "Sounds like we have a good lead. Tell us, where can we find the man responsible for killing our troops?" Ishaan motioned with his hand once more and the archer who had targeted the woman previously pulled the bowstring back once again, this time pointing the arrow at Cylos's father.

Cylos instinctively flinched in the direction of the assailant, desperate to do something, anything to help his father. He had half a mind to jump right through the gaps in the stable and charge at the archer, if nothing else to serve as a distraction. But before he could do anything rash, a large hand firmly grasped his shoulder, pulling him back.

"I won't let them harm your father, Cylos," Belza said. "I will intervene, but before I do, I need your help. There isn't much time to explain, but I have a plan. How would you like to ride my alcier again?"

Despite efforts to play it coy, Cylos couldn't prevent a sharp inhale of excitement from escaping his mouth. "I'll do whatever you need, Belza," he managed to say, regaining his composure.

"Good. It's a little risky, but I think it's our best chance. You'll need to be brave, Cylos, but my alcier will know what to do. I'm confident it will keep you safe. Are you up for the task, Cylos?"

The uncertainty of it all caused a momentary surge of fright to swell in Cylos's chest, but he didn't show it with his defiant response. "You can count on me for anything," he said.

"Good, there isn't much time to explain. I'm going to cast my alcier in here so it's ready, and you need to climb aboard. I can command it telepathically. All you need to do is hold on." Belza didn't wait for a response. Instead, using the light of the sun entering the side of the stable, Belza held up his hands with the fingers spread wide, projecting a shadow onto the wall that reminded Cylos of a pair of antlers. Within moments, the familiar alcier materialized, and Belza stepped toward it, placing a hand against its face and bringing his forehead to it as if urging it to remain quiet.

Cylos watched as the two locked eyes, then without Belza uttering a word, the wide-antlered creature dropped to its knees so Cylos could get on. At a gesture from Belza, Cylos scrambled aboard, then the shadow creature stood to its full height.

There was so much Cylos wanted to ask Belza, but his reeling thoughts were interrupted when his attention was pulled back to the conversation outside. While he and Belza chatted, Cylos had noticed the sound of his father speaking in the background, but he hadn't heard the specifics. But Ishaan's words came through loud and clear.

"I've heard enough excuses and stalling. Tell me, it was Matthias, right? People of Fillenglen, does Matthias have any family here in town? A wife or children perhaps? Because if so, I think we've found our new candidate for the first to die if the caster isn't turned over to us immediately."

The man who had talked against Cylos's father spoke up again. "He sure does. A wife and son. Why don't we show you to his house if he won't cooperate?"

"Why don't *you* shut your mouth, Nedric, you pile of scum." It was Lorcan who spoke up this time. His defiant tone against Cylos's father's detractor brought a satisfied smile to Cylos's face. "You'd willingly turn over an innocent woman and child to these intruders rather than stand alongside our compatriot Matthias? You're a disgrace."

"No one who supports *casters*, especially putting the rest of us in danger, is a compatriot of mine," the man called Nedric hissed.

Lorcan and Nedric's comments sparked a series of arguments on both sides as some came to the defense of Lorcan and Matthias while others demanded the safety of the collective village be prioritized no matter the individual sacrifice. From what Cylos gathered, those in the latter line of thinking weren't just willing but eager to preserve Fillenglen by turning in a caster.

"Alright, my patience has run out!" Ishaan shouted with a sneer to interrupt their bickering. "We'll find our friend Matthias's family soon enough. For now, since you all insist on wasting our time rather than revealing the caster, so you'll know we're serious, we'll start with our original plan." He then gestured to the archer, who pointed his arrow at the woman from before and pulled back the bowstring.

As she ducked while letting out a second scream, Belza whispered, "Be brave, Cylos. I must go now." Then, without a second glance, Belza burst out of the stable entrance, trotting toward the invaders.

CHAPTER 7
THE FROZEN LAKE

Stand down! Don't harm her or anyone else. I'm the one you seek," Belza bellowed at the onlookers as he made his storming approach. As far as Cylos could see, though his view was admittedly limited now atop the alcier as he strained to look through the gaps in the stable wall, every single head turned toward Belza. A tense silence ensued.

Placing himself directly between the Fillenglen villagers and their aggressors, Belza pulled back his deer hide coat, and although Cylos could only see his back, given the wide-eyed gasps that followed, he was positive the old hermit had revealed his caster beam.

Cylos was surprised to see Belza's mace and throwing hatchets still strapped to his back and side. He didn't look prepared to defend himself, but perhaps he had other ideas.

"You were correct. I am a shadow caster," Belza began. "But I only acted in defense against your troops who attacked me. All I wanted was to be left in peace. I have no desire to hurt anyone, so I will grant you the same opportunity I gave your gang last night. Leave me be and depart from Fillenglen, and no harm will come to you. That is all I ask. I do not wish to partake in any bloodshed."

Ishaan scoffed and opened his mouth to speak when his leader, the red-haired man with the double swords crossing his back, extended an arm to silence him. Ishaan shut his mouth before nodding respectfully and pulling his black and gray horse a couple paces backward.

The man Ishaan had introduced as Thaddeus Ralkentin bore his cold eyes into Belza, then a wicked smile spread across his face. "Well now, who would have thought I'd be so fortunate? I know who you are, caster. You're an exact match of the description I received from Sentinalia."

Cylos's eyes widened as Belza's head dropped ever so slightly. It was precisely as he'd feared.

Thaddeus continued. "You messed with the wrong family in Sentinalia. There's a price on your head so big, I could give every one of my troops a comfortable life by bringing you in. Who could've guessed my plans for Fillenglen would overlap with such a massive bounty? You claim you don't want bloodshed, well, then why don't you surrender? We'll be taking you with us one way or the other. You get to choose how difficult it is. Don't make us punish this village for your obstinance."

"Yeah," the man called Nedric yelled out. "If you truly want to be noble, turn yourself in and leave us alone. That's the best way you can protect us from them."

Cylos heard his father scoff. "Nedric, if you think thugs like these will keep their word and leave us alone after they've gotten the caster, you're more foolish than I thought." His tone was more disappointed than accusatory. "Don't listen to them, Belza. We'll fight alongside you to defend our village."

"No, Matthias," Belza replied sternly. "Ishaan spoke true about one thing. You aren't cut out for this fight. Move all your people to safety. These men will only treat you as targets to slaughter to try to convince me to stop fighting. I won't allow that. You must trust me. I will defend the village. I won't allow harm to come to a single one of you." Belza then removed his mace from his back and held it defensively, as if daring Thaddeus Ralkentin and the others to charge him.

But instead, Thaddeus and Ishaan shared a glance then both started chuckling.

"You're hopelessly outnumbered, old man. Even for a caster," said Ralkentin.

"I've heard that before," Belza retorted stiffly.

Cylos's breath caught in his throat. The tension hanging in the air was palpable. Belza gripped his mace tighter as the two enemy leaders watched him through narrowed eyes, holding perfectly still in cautious anticipation. Who would strike first?

Cylos heard his father and Lorcan indistinctly ushering people to shelter. He imagined his father felt heartbroken stepping aside while Belza took on all the risk, but figured he was also wise enough to trust Belza in the face of such a daunting threat. He was better off hiding than pointlessly sacrificing himself in a conflict where he'd only be getting in Belza's way.

Just when Cylos thought the tense stalemate would last forever, Belza made a subtle move, turning his head to one side toward Cylos. It had been discreet, but Cylos took it as a sign. He leaned his chest into the back of the alcier's neck and threw his arms around it to get a tight grip, feeling its cushy fur press against his chest and the softness of its hide on his cheek.

With a flick of his hand, Ishaan signaled to the archer, who immediately raised his bow and fired a shot at Belza. Ishaan and Thaddeus must have also detected Belza's slight motion and felt uncomfortable with it.

Cylos took a sharp inhale as he watched in terror, but, with his mace held at the ready, Belza blocked the incoming arrow with little effort and it ricocheted away harmlessly. Responding with unbelievable speed, Belza pulled a throwing hatchet from his side and hurled it right back at the archer. The man had no time to dodge. A wide-eyed look of petrified horror was the last Cylos saw of him before he toppled off his horse.

But Cylos had no time to admire Belza's expert maneuver, nor see what retaliation the bandits would unleash on Belza next, for the instant the archer dropped to the snow, the alcier lowered its head and charged forward with impressive agility. Its antlers burst through the side of the stable, sending splintered wood flying as it crashed through the wall and sprinted to the northeast away from the battle. Despite his secure hold, Cylos was still caught off guard by the alcier's reaction, which took his breath away and nearly caused him to slip off. He increased his grip, pressing even tighter into the antlered creature's neck.

After breaking through the side of the stable and hearing a few powerful footsteps from the alcier's dashing hooves, a call came from behind that sounded like Thaddeus Ralkentin.

"That's a… that's a shadow creature. There must be another caster!"

Another caster? The words rang in Cylos's head. *They think* I'm *a caster?*

"Quick, Ishaan, take some troops and stop him. I'll deal with the old man," Thaddeus said.

Despite the alcier's speed and Cylos's fear of losing hold, he managed to pry his head off the creature long enough to look behind him and see nearly half the horsemen take off in pursuit. Was this Belza's plan? To trick them into thinking Cylos was a second caster? He'd given Cylos no instruction whatsoever, so he hoped Belza's declaration would hold true that the alcier knew what to do while he held on for dear life.

Still looking over his shoulder, Cylos also realized Belza had taken advantage of the momentary chaos. His mace was now stuck in the snow beside him and he had once again summoned his leviakhus and a shadow crossbow before any further retaliation could come his way. The last Cylos saw, the leviakhus was diving into the snow and Belza was firing off bolts with the crossbow while Thaddeus Ralkentin called out orders and organized his men into position. A few of them fired desperate shots at the Fillenglen villagers, but Cylos was relieved that, as far as he could see, his father's efforts to move them to safety were successful and none were harmed.

Cylos momentarily worried that perhaps Nedric and some of the others who opposed casters might seek to aid Ralkentin by sneaking an attack on Belza from behind. He shook off the thought, instead presuming they'd be too cowardly and would instead take shelter until the conflict was over rather than risk bringing harm to themselves from either side. Now the question was if Belza could truly protect the village on his own. He had fared well against the thieves outside his cabin, but he was up against a far larger and more skilled force this time. Cylos struggled to feel optimistic but did his best to hold out hope for his elderly friend.

Besides, he had his own problems to worry about. Cylos's thoughts shifted from Belza to his own situation as he watched Ishaan and the other troops chasing him. Some fired arrows at Cylos, but the alcier sped on with incredible speed and grace, keeping them well out of range. Daring to look forward again, Cylos tried to get his bearings and determine where the alcier was headed. It took a moment, but when realization struck Cylos, he couldn't suppress a gasp.

The alcier was headed straight for the frozen lake outside the village. And judging by its speed, it had no intention of altering course.

"I hope you know what you're doing," Cylos cried.

The alcier let out a bellowing snort that Cylos had no idea how to interpret.

Reaching the shore, the alcier leaped over a row of snow-covered rocks and Cylos slammed his eyes shut while airborne. When he heard the hooves settle down again and begin beating against a solid surface, he was relieved to realize the creature hadn't crashed through. The ice had held.

The alcier continued at an only slightly slower pace, unable to find the same solid footing on the icy lake, when Cylos heard a voice from behind him.

"Keep going, we're gaining. We can catch him on the ice. Don't let the caster get away!" Ishaan cried.

Cylos swung his head around to see the line of horsemen enter the icy surface as well. He shouldn't have been surprised. The temperatures had been so cold the Fillenglen villagers took mounts and weighty loads across the ice all the time for fishing. Still, he'd hoped his pursuers would be deterred or that perhaps the ice would give way for them where it hadn't for the single alcier. Hopefully their complete lack of reluctance at crossing the lake hadn't dashed whatever plan Belza and the alcier intended.

They'd gone about halfway across the lake when the alcier shifted its head to the side as if looking back, then after letting out a low grunt, it skidded to a halt. Cylos gave a surprised shout as the alcier slid forward on the ice before turning around to face the incoming horses.

"What? What are you doing?" Cylos exclaimed. But the alcier gave no response this time. As Cylos leaned to his right so he could see both the advancing enemies and the side of the alcier's face, he thought he saw a determination in the shadow beast's right eye that he didn't know could exist in such a creature.

"It stopped. Bring it down," Ishaan called as the horses picked up speed. They still had a gap to close, but Cylos could feel nervous sweat dripping down his forehead upon realizing they'd be upon them in a matter of seconds. A few arrows flew their way, and Cylos struggled to hold on as the alcier swung its head side to side, expertly deflecting the incoming projectiles with its massive antlers.

And yet still it stood its ground, leaving Cylos aghast and mystified at what it was intending. Despite knowing full well inquiries were futile, Cylos was about to question it out loud again when, without warning, it rose up on its back legs.

Cylos's breath caught in his throat and he struggled to hold on, clutching for the creature's shaggy neck hair, as the alcier nearly bucked him off with the unexpected backward jerk. The shadow beast kicked its front feet in the air a few times, then brought its full weight back down with incredible force, smashing its hooves into the ice below it.

When its hooves struck the ice, not only was there a physical impact, but a sharp line of shadow shot straight forward from each hoof, cutting through the ice layer in front of them like scythes. As the shadowy substance sliced through the frozen surface, an unsettling cracking noise sounded out ahead of Cylos.

No Tangible Realm creature could have had such an immediate effect on the thick ice.

The alcier didn't wait to see what would happen next. Instead, it reared up again, bringing its hooves down a second time, sending two more blasts of dark shadow. This time the cracks became visible as the ice in front of the shadow creature split sharply, sending sprays of cold water shooting up between the gaps, which were as wide as Cylos's forearms were long.

A web of cracking ice weaved toward Ishaan and the other horsemen. Despite the panic on their faces, there was little they could do. Soon cracks surrounded them and the ice began crumbling under their weight. Cylos watched with his mouth agape as the first horse went down, sinking into the freezing water, its rider slipping off beside it. The horse whinnied in panic and the man let out a scream until it was cut off abruptly as he hit the arctic water.

"Keep going, hurry!" Ishaan shrieked. He must have realized turning back was futile and their only hope of escape was to reach the alcier before more ice gave way beneath them.

But after a third strike to the ice from the alcier's hooves, once again blasting shadowy rays along with it, the ice's fidelity gave way. The shockwave this time sent the ice shattering in all directions on the half of the lake in front of Cylos. All the horses behind Ishaan fell through, a chorus of whinnies and panicked screams following them.

The toppled horses, thinking only of their own survival, desperately paddled to the side, eager to get to solid ice. Many found their footing and darted away across the icy lake, escaping its surface to the far banks. Their riders weren't so lucky. Even those who could swim well wouldn't last long in the frigid water, particularly those pinned under large blocks of ice.

Somehow after it all, Ishaan's gray and black horse stayed upright, leaping from ice chunk to ice chunk, narrowly dodging breaking rifts of cracked ice that should have sent both mount and rider plunging into the freezing water. As Ishaan drew nearer, Cylos realized he was going to reach them. Ishaan held a spear at the ready, poised to attack. Would the alcier strike the ice again? Or turn and run? Should Cylos grab the sword off his back and prepare to defend himself?

Right as Ishaan was nearly upon them, the alcier lowered its head, pointing its massive antlers at the incoming foe. Cylos saw Ishaan hesitate but he had no time to react. From out of the shadow spirals on either of the alcier's antlers shot a wave of tangled, misty tendrils. The black, purple, and dark gray blast landed directly in front of Ishaan's horse. The impact sent an explosion of ice and water that dropped the mount and rider instantly, sending them careening into the water below. Ishaan let out a frightened yell that was silenced by a booming splash. Once they'd plummeted, the alcier didn't wait around. It turned and sprinted toward the opposite shore of the icy lake.

Cylos couldn't believe what he had witnessed. He felt like he barely breathed the entire time to the opposite shore. Once the alcier reached solid ground again, he let out a heavy exhale, though the feeling of shock was still like a clamp on his heart.

The alcier then turned left and began running around the northwest end of the lake, heading back toward Fillenglen, no doubt eager to return to its master's side. As it sprinted, Cylos took in the scene of the lake beside him. The riderless horses either stood on the far shore or ran off in the opposite direction. He saw no sign of any of their masters anywhere, save for one.

A solitary steed vaulted from the frozen depths, its black head appearing first, followed by its gray body and black legs, its hooves finding purchase on solid ice once more before trotting to the far eastern shore. Whether fate was on his side or his skill truly matched his bravado, there atop the resilient mount, amidst the shimmering expanse of the frozen lake, clung an unmistakable figure in his round and pointed helmet. Ishaan.

For a second, Cylos thought Ishaan might turn and give pursuit. But whether clinging to life and desperate to find warmth or intending to meet up with his troops at a predetermined location, the last Cylos saw of Ishaan, he was galloping away in the opposite direction, leaving the icy lake and the departing alcier behind.

If this had been Belza's plan, it had worked to perfection. In desperate pursuit of a decoy caster, nearly half of Thaddeus Ralkentin's mounted troops had been vanquished without Cylos lifting a finger.

Regaining his composure at last, Cylos spoke to the alcier. "That was incredible. You were amazing."

But the alcier didn't respond, instead it carried on at a determined speed like before, its powerful hooves thumping against the snow-packed ground. Cylos didn't know how to explain it, but something about the alcier's sharp focus and lack of acknowledgment felt off, as if it were overtaken by a fresh wave of uneasiness.

Perhaps it was little wonder why. Between the other horsemen and the dozens of foot soldiers back at the village, Belza would be wildly outnumbered.

As the alcier pressed on, the wind whipping in Cylos's face, Cylos couldn't ignore the pit forming in his stomach. His intuition told him Belza was in trouble. Cylos could only hope whatever scheme Belza had devised for dealing with the rest of his foes could yet turn out as successful as the alcier ploy.

CHAPTER 8

DESPERATE MEASURES

Cylos heard the conflict outside the village before he saw it. Littered among the human shouting was the occasional guttural screech Cylos could only assume belonged to the leviakhus. He supposed the noise was a good sign. It meant Belza was still in the fight. Hopefully the return of the alcier would be enough to end it.

But once Cylos caught sight of the distant scene producing the noise, a lump formed in his throat, and he let out an audible gasp. From what he could tell, Thaddeus Ralkentin's troops had their hands full. Several of them laid vanquished, their bodies strewn about the snow-covered ground, but the reason for Belza's apparent success left Cylos aghast.

It wasn't only Belza and the leviakhus in combat. Atop the galloping alcier, Cylos could see two other shadow creatures—the euobiloceros and another he didn't recognize—in the fray along with the caster.

What was Belza doing? Hadn't he just told Cylos it was unsafe to summon more than two shadow creatures at a time? Had that been an exaggeration? Or was the caster taking a serious risk? Was this why the alcier had become unsettled? Had it sensed its master summoning more casts than he had the strength for? To use Belza's own words—spreading himself too thin?

His mind spinning with questions, Cylos studied the commotion before him. Bursting out of a recently dug snow burrow, the dark green form of the leviakhus emerged in force. It grabbed hold of a hapless foot soldier in its jaws and tossed the man aside effortlessly, though its movements were far slower than the night before. As it attempted to assail a group of archers, it became apparent why. Several spears and arrows protruded from its underbelly.

On the other side of the battlefield, Belza's euobiloceros went charging at a pair of horsemen, its head lowered, ready to strike with menacing horns. But it too appeared slow and wounded, its movements stumbling and woozy.

The third shadow cast stood in front of Belza. It was a bulky creature, like a flat-faced bear standing on two legs. Belza was down on one knee behind it, firing shots with his crossbow. The large-bellied, bear-like creature served as a shield, threatening any who dared approach Belza, but it had wounds of its own and Cylos cringed at the sight of two arrows protruding from Belza as well, one out of his side and the other from his leg.

Despite the dire situation, Cylos found hope in the enemy's dwindled numbers and what appeared to be a still unscathed village. With the arrival of the alcier to provide further reinforcement, perhaps the tide would turn for good and Belza would yet rise victorious.

But fate mocked Cylos's attempts at optimism. The leviakhus burst out of the snow and a bold fighter rolled to dodge its upward surge, then landed a precise upward slash with a curved sword that sliced a vertical gash up the creature's neck. The legged serpent let out a shrill cry before toppling over sideways. Wispy tendrils of black and purple shadow began rising from it as its body slowly faded from existence.

Immediately after, the euobiloceros landed a charge that sent two men flying, but a mounted woman rode past and leapt from her horse to land atop the shadow beast's back. She slammed her lance down hard, burying the weapon into its neck. The euobiloceros gave out a weak grunt, then slumped to the ground. Its body began to dematerialize like the leviakhus's.

As if matters hadn't already taken a turn for the worst, Cylos watched in horror as three horsemen bearing torches sprinted past the fading euobiloceros, headed straight for the nearest house. They were going to set it ablaze!

Belza must have seen them as well, but pinned behind the bear-like creature as projectiles flew his way, he would never make it in time. Cylos bit the inside of his cheek, watching in helpless suspense. Belza had tucked his shadow crossbow beneath his arm but Cylos wasn't sure why. It only took a moment to figure out, though, as a fresh swirl of misty tendrils appeared in front of Belza, from which flew a black and purple avian shadow creature with a bright orange beak.

Another shadow creature? Cylos ground his teeth together. He hoped Belza knew what he was doing.

The eagle-like shadow beast darted toward the torch-bearing riders with astounding speed. Cylos had thought nothing could prevent the horsemen from reaching the village and setting Fillenglen ablaze. But in a lightning flash the avian covered the distance.

When the bird got in close to the horsemen, it hovered in the air and batted its wings swiftly. The repeated motions sent blasts of wind at the riders that not only extinguished their flames, but also knocked one of the riders off his mount, toppling into the other. The house they targeted was spared.

Cylos wondered if perhaps this tactic was indicative of what Belza had faced all throughout the conflict. When Ralkentin's troops spread the battlefield wider than Belza and the leviakhus could handle, perhaps the caster had been forced to desperately summon more creatures to prevent similar threats on the village. Now Cylos wished Belza had allowed his father and the other villagers to help. Perhaps some would have been killed, but they could have alleviated the pressure on Belza rather than leaving it all in his hands.

The eagle-like creature then swooped down and subdued the two riders it had knocked over, but as it took off again, it became an easy target for surviving troops despite its speed. Though it unleashed successful attacks of wind and shadow mist on a few more bandits, a barrage of timely arrows soon sent it cascading to the ground, dissipating like the others. Belza must have chosen it mainly for speed, not durability.

What had looked like a battle still leaning in Belza's favor had rapidly shifted with the consecutive defeats of the three shadow creatures. That also meant Belza now had three casts in a recovery state in the Shadow Realm, which he'd described as a risky prospect in and of itself. That wasn't considering the alcier and bear-like cast still summoned in the Tangible Realm.

"Come on, alcier, we've got to get down there. Belza needs us." Cylos intended his shout to be encouraging, but the antlered shadow creature acted more perturbed than motivated. It snorted, as if only then remembering Cylos was on its back. To Cylos's surprise, it slowed its pace, then turned its head back toward him and gave him a stiff nudge with its snout while leaning to one side.

"Hey!" Cylos called, but it was no use. The alcier pushed him off its back, where he fell gently in the snow, then it returned to its blazing pace to enter the fray. Cylos smacked the snow in front of him as he let out a groan, but soon realized the alcier was only trying to protect him, perhaps heeding a subconscious command from its master. Cylos could almost hear Belza's voice saying, *You wouldn't be safe on the alcier's back. I can handle this battle by myself.*

Pulling himself up, Cylos shuffled through the snow after the alcier. He considered sprinting after it to insert himself into the battle. Belza needed all the help he could get. But then he thought twice. He had no experience in combat and would only get in the way. It would be best to keep his distance to avoid interfering against Belza's wishes or making matters worse. He told himself he'd stay alert, though, and if he saw any opportunity to jump in, he would. At the very least, he was determined to move within striking distance, keeping a close eye on the proceedings as he advanced.

Among the survivors, Cylos finally identified Thaddeus Ralkentin, though somewhere in combat he must have lost his horse. With his double swords drawn, he stepped forward from the crowd of troops firing in Belza's direction and charged at the bear-like creature and the caster it protected. Belza fired shadowy bolts at the lead bandit, but Thaddeus expertly dodged or deflected each one. Belza's movement between shots was labored, as if every painstaking motion took all his energy. It reminded Cylos of someone struggling through sticky mud, Belza's former fluidity and precision abandoning him.

The alcier, meanwhile, must have thought Belza and the other cast could hold their own against Thaddeus Ralkentin, and identified the remaining survivors as the bigger threat. The two groups responsible for defeating the leviakhus, euobiloceros, and eagle cast had now congregated into one large force. The alcier didn't arrive a moment too soon, for the survivors looked poised to either march on Belza to back up Ralkentin, or charge Fillenglen, but instead their attention was captured by the antlered beast.

Uninhibited by wounds, the alcier appeared fresh and prepared for combat, catching several bandits off guard as it blasted shadow from its antlers and knocked fighters to the ground with streaks of shadow from its hooves as they crashed into the snow-packed earth. Cylos was confident the alcier would fare well against the tired bandits, so his attention returned to Belza.

Once Thaddeus got in close to the caster, he first had the tall shadow creature to deal with, but he appeared undeterred. The bulky, bear-like creature brought a massive fist down to the snow, aiming to crush the gang's leader, but Ralkentin dodged out of the way, then unleashed a crossways slice with both his swords on the creature's wrist. It let out a loud groan, then lowered its other fist, but Thaddeus met this one with a high strike of his swords before the blow could land. As the creature jerked its hand up in a pained recoil, Thaddeus went for its left leg with yet another devastating cut.

The bear gave out a groan and toppled to one knee. As it fell, Belza attempted a shot with his crossbow, but Thaddeus was too fast again, rolling out of the way before delivering a final blow to the bear-like shadow cast with a crossways swipe from both swords to its belly. The beast moaned as it fell face-first into the snow, and wisps of its body started rising and disappearing in vapory tendrils.

Cylos's heartbeat quickened. His once-measured pace turned into a sprint, adrenaline surging through his veins. A quick glance to his right revealed the alcier dealing with the last remaining troops of Ralkentin's band, but the shadow creature was surrounded, leaving it too occupied to come to Belza's aid. Cylos was the only reinforcement the old caster had.

Stepping out from behind the disappearing form of the bear-like creature Belza had been hiding behind, the old hermit bore a dark battle axe. The misty tendrils following its every movement revealed its nature as a newly casted shadow weapon. The axe was even larger than the mace Belza had carried previously, but he wielded it with equal ease. The old man still had some fight left in him.

Thaddeus jumped over the disappearing shadow creature and brought both swords careening toward Belza. The caster parried with his axe, a combination of sparks and shadowy vapor shooting from each respective weapon. But Thaddeus didn't look the least bit intimidated. Instead, he spun back then swiped again, staying on the offensive with each strike. Belza continued to parry, but his movements grew slower and slower, every motion a greater struggle.

Cylos had just arrived within earshot when he heard Thaddeus say, "You're slow, old man. Much slower than other casters I've killed. You're lucky you had your wretched creatures to protect you or this would've never been a contest to begin with." Then, without giving Belza any chance to respond, Ralkentin feinted to his left, causing Belza to swing the axe, only to return to his right and deliver a crushing swipe to Belza's stomach.

"Noooo!" Cylos yelled, unable to restrain himself. He pulled the sword out of the scabbard on his back, gripping the black- and gold-streaked hilt as tightly as he could. He had no idea what he was doing, but he was determined to do something.

His shout caused Thaddeus to look up from the form of Belza, who toppled to one side in the snow, his battle axe crashing to the ground and disappearing in a tangle of shadowy tendrils. Thaddeus stepped over the old caster and walked two more paces forward.

"So, the other little caster survived, huh? Foolish of you to come back, young one."

Cylos's eyes narrowed and his brow furrowed, wrath unlike any he'd ever experienced boiled inside him until he felt heat coming off his face.

"You fell for the bait. I'm *not* a caster," he said through gritted teeth, holding his sword at the ready. Fear gripped his chest and throat, but he still forced out the words. "But no longer will I sit back idly. I will always, *always* come to their defense."

Thaddeus scoffed. "So, you were a distraction then, huh? Pathetic.

The only thing worse than casters are the lonrelmians who support them. Good thing you'll never grow up to do anything with your misguided ideals." Then, with the same speed he'd used against Belza, Thaddeus swiped his blood-stained swords at Cylos. The boy was shocked when he somehow blocked the first two blows, though the vibration of the metal of Thaddeus's blades against his own sent painful shockwaves down his hands. His inexperience soon overcame his fortune when, with a third sideways blow, Thaddeus hit Cylos's sword and sent it flying out of his grip.

Cylos's wrath was overwhelmed by dread as he backed away, feeling helpless as Thaddeus approached with his double blades at the ready. For the second time in as many days, Cylos was certain his life was over. What had made him think he could do anything to help? Why hadn't he stayed hidden?

Right as he was about to despair, he heard a roar so loud and crazed he swore it had come from a shadow creature. To his disbelief, the bleeding form of Belza appeared right behind Thaddeus Ralkentin. Before the lead bandit could react, Belza hit him hard in the back with an upward swing of his Tangible Realm mace, sending the man sprawling forward with a panicked scream.

Thaddeus must have thought Belza was dead or at least down for the count. Cylos couldn't blame him; he'd thought the same. But the old hulk of a man had proven indomitable yet again. Although after delivering this blow, Belza collapsed to his back in the snow yet again and Cylos dashed to his side.

But before he could speak or attend to him, Thaddeus let out an enraged growl. He looked badly hurt, but with Belza far from full strength, it was no surprise the old caster hadn't managed to finish him off. Cylos turned toward Thaddeus to see him staggering to his feet, brandishing the two swords like a man possessed.

"I should have made sure you were dead, caster scum," he growled. "I won't make the same mistake twice." But as he lifted a leg to step forward, his retaliation was interrupted by the sound of hoofbeats. Thaddeus turned in time to see Belza's alcier galloping straight for him.

He met its lowered antlers with his swords, stopping its advance even though it pushed his feet backward, skidding in the snow as he braced himself. The alcier then shook its head back and forth, attempting to beat Thaddeus into submission. But each time he blocked the antlers with his blades, even landing a few strikes against the alcier.

At last, the alcier backed up and let out a bellowing grunt, lowering its head for a second charge.

"It didn't work last time and it won't work this time," Thaddeus taunted with a scoff, holding his swords in the same defensive position as before. But rather than rush him, the alcier used the same tactic Cylos had witnessed at the lake, blasting a surge of shadowy mist from the shadow spirals on either antler. Thaddeus held out his crossed blades to block it, but the impact still forced him backward, knocking him on his back into the snow where he lost grip on his swords as they tumbled over his head.

Flipping over, he crawled desperately toward the fallen blades, but before he could reach them, he looked back over his shoulder to find the alcier right above him, its front hooves raised high in the air.

"No!" he cried out, rolling the rest of the way over onto his back and throwing his arms over his face in a futile attempt at defense. His cry was silenced by the impact of the alcier's descending hooves crushing his ribs with a sickening crunch, smashing Thaddeus into the snow as a fresh set of scythe-like shadows cut into the defeated bandit's chest and neck before slicing forward into the snow beyond.

When Cylos finally exhaled, it felt like he hadn't breathed in hours. And it was only then he noticed his breathing sounded deafening in the eerie stillness. The alcier must have finished off the remaining troops or sent them retreating before charging Thaddeus Ralkentin, for not a single living soul among their enemies remained on the battlefield.

Belza's words to Cylos's father had rung true. With the help of his shadow creatures, Belza had defeated the foes and defended the village.

Cylos's full attention returned to Belza as he crouched beside him. His breathing was shallow, his eyes looked glazed and distant, and his eyelids were drooping. Cylos couldn't bring himself to look at the arrow wounds or, worse, the severely bleeding gash from Thaddeus's blades. "Belza... You're hurt badly. Can you summon your panghordra now? Either way, I'll go get my mom. She'll be able to mend you. You'll be okay." The words poured out of his mouth in a desperate panic as he struggled to convince himself they were true.

When Belza didn't respond, Cylos started to stand up, intending to run to his house and shout for his mom, but before he could, Belza's hand shot up and grabbed Cylos's wrist.

"No, Cylos. It's no use," he whispered. "It's too late."

"But, but your panghordra... you said..."

"I know what I said. But I've already overextended myself. Remember when I told you it was dangerous to cast more than two shadows at a time? I did what I had to do, but the damage I've caused myself is far more profound than what's visible from Ralkentin's swords. His attack had no additional bearing on the consequence I'd already doomed myself to. With four shadows in a recovery state and my alcier still summoned, I'm afraid even attempting to call forth the panghordra would do me in."

As if on cue, the alcier limped over to Belza, crouching to the ground and nuzzling its snout and forehead into Belza's cheek.

"Then send the alcier back to the Shadow Realm, too, so you can both recover, and then let my mom take a look at you. It's worth a shot." Cylos was speaking of things he didn't fully understand, but he didn't care. He refused to accept the situation was hopeless even though cold tears traced down his cheeks.

Belza exhaled sharply in what sounded like his closest attempt at a chuckle. "I admire your optimism, Cylos, but you must trust me. Never have I been required to put my life at such risk by calling on so many creatures at once, but had I gone about things any other way, innocents in Fillenglen would have been harmed. Instead, all have gone unscathed. It is an honor for me to use my skills to defend you, your family, and your village, even at so great a cost."

Cylos didn't like what Belza was insinuating, but he kept quiet.

Belza gave out a wheezing cough. "Now, I would task you with one last thing." He spoke in a whisper between raspy breaths. "All my supplies are yours... but there are three I ask you keep safe... The first is a book... The second is a small tool I forged... silver with two pointed ends and springs... activated by a circular switch. The last is a talisman—

you'll know it when you see it... It's a gold hexagon with a translucent gray stone in the center... I'm trusting them all... to you."

Belza let in a labored, gasping inhale and Cylos placed a delicate hand on his shoulder.

"You can count on me, Belza. I'll take good care of them. What are they for?"

Belza's eyelids drooped further and Cylos felt more tears rushing down his cheeks. They felt like shards of ice carving lines down his face in the bitter Fillenglen wind.

"I... don't have... the strength... I trust you'll have... the wisdom... to use them for the right purposes... at the right time."

"No," Cylos began. "No, Belza, no, hang on. I'll... I'll go get help. You can't... you still have to teach me how to use the sword you forged for me. I want to see more of your shadow creatures, to ride your alcier again. I want to hear about Sentinalia. Please, Belza, please..."

The corners of Belza's lips perked up in a feeble attempt to smile. He brought one hand to Cylos's face, the other to the alcier's muzzle.

"I know you'll... make me proud, Cylos. Malgar needs... more lonrelmians... like you."

Belza's eyes closed, and Cylos could barely make out the whispered words he attempted to recite.

Should an... evil arise
I pledge to... eliminate it
To this end I give my life

I will be a keeper... of... peace
A friend... to all
Defender... virtue
Seeker... solutions
An ally... of justice

I am a shadow caster... and this is my pledge

The old man's fingertips traced against Cylos's face and both his hands dropped. The alcier let out a pathetic pained whimper while nuzzling into its master for what Cylos realized would be the final time. A tangle of shadowy tendrils then emerged around the antlered beast, swirling in all directions, until it dissipated from view.

Belza was gone.

Cylos's breath caught in his throat for an instant, then the tears flowed unabated. Behind his choked sobs, Cylos hardly heard the Fillenglen villagers departing the safety of their homes and letting out cheers of joy at their deliverance, hardly heard his parents call his name as they ran toward him, hardly heard his own heart beating.

They were all an afterthought next to the man who had just given his life. All of them were alive and safe because of Belza. Because he'd stayed and fought rather than flee when he had no obligation to do so.

Belza was the greatest and noblest man Cylos had ever known. How anyone could side with the likes of Thaddeus Ralkentin and Ishaan Nikanti over a selfless shadow caster like Belza was beyond Cylos's comprehension.

Cylos's father had always spoken highly of shadow casters. Belza was the only shadow caster Cylos had ever known, but in their short time together, he'd shown Cylos enough to confirm his father's praise. Cylos knew where his support lied. Regardless of what lonrelmian fear and greed had enacted into law, to his core he was firmly rooted on the side of shadow casters.

With tears streaming down his face as he stared at the lifeless form of Belza, he swore to himself that no matter the cost, he'd spend the rest of his life defending their cause.

PART TWO
LUCRATIVE DELIVERY

CHAPTER 9

PERLATUM

Five years had passed since the day Belza gave his life for the people of Fillenglen, but not a day passed that Cylos hadn't thought of it. Lost in his thoughts as he rode his trotting horse, he remembered thinking someday the constant hollow knot in his stomach from how deeply he missed the old hermit would disappear.

But if the last years were any indication, perhaps he was wrong. Every time he rode his horse, all he could think about was the rush of excitement he felt atop Belza's alcier. In the years since the incident, he'd become an expert rider, a feeble attempt to recapture the invigoration he once enjoyed aboard the shadow mount.

Cylos and his parents hadn't stayed long in Fillenglen after Belza's death. While there was undeniable gratitude across Fillenglen for the part Belza played in protecting the village, it didn't change the reality that casting was against the law. And Cylos's father had made his loyalties clear in his support of Belza.

To make matters worse, Cylos's role as a decoy had sparked a rumor that the boy actually was a caster. Although untrue, it remained a dangerous association. The Phetos family had been widely beloved in Fillenglen, but some were so vehemently dedicated to following the laws against shadow casting that Matthias and Tilly's reputation as caster supporters put them at risk. Fear about what could come to them if they remained as known pro-casters in the small town led them to depart. Cylos was sad but hadn't disagreed with the decision. He saw no alternative.

With the help of Lorcan and his family, a few nights after Belza's death, Cylos and his parents had left their home in Fillenglen behind, taking only necessities with them, including of course the book, tool, and talisman Belza had entrusted to Cylos.

He kept the three items close at hand at all times. He'd thumbed through the book several times since receiving it from Belza and found it fascinating, containing dozens of sketches and examples of the shadow casts Belza knew how to summon. Regarding the tool and the talisman, though, he had yet to find out what they were for or how they were used.

The tool was kept in a small leather sheath lined with fur because it had two razor-sharp horizontal edges, ending in a point. They could be spring loaded toward each other so they were parallel, then activated to snap back to their flat, horizontal starting point with startling speed by pressing a circular switch at the bottom where the two hinging ends connected.

Cylos had played with it several times but, outside of nearly losing a finger, had never determined a use. Among his final words, Belza expressed hope that Cylos would know what to do with all of them when the time was right. Cylos often found himself wondering if he ever would and wished the hermit had found the strength to tell him more.

Leaving Fillenglen had been a difficult transition for the Phetos family. Cylos's father had lived there his whole life, never intending to leave behind the house and farm he'd inherited from his parents. Cylos's mother especially missed the comforts of their home, the lovely décor, furniture, and adornments she'd put so much work into. Lorcan promised he'd keep track of it for them, in case they returned. But Cylos wasn't sure any of them believed they ever would. They all missed Lorcan and other dear neighbors and friends. At least their horses, ox, and dog had joined them, but in most ways they'd been forced to start anew, rebuilding a home and life far from their comfortable norms.

Their departure took them southwest where they settled in the small town of Wentsling, considered part of Malgar's Far Western Shores, though it was over an hour's ride from the region's main and much larger coastal city of Perlatum, Cylos's current destination.

As the tops of Perlatum's tall metal and glass buildings dotting the sandy shore came into view in the distance over the ridge Cylos climbed, he forced himself to refocus. He'd been so lost in his thoughts he hadn't realized how far he'd traveled. Perlatum was a global hub for imports and exports, thus it was heavily guarded with strict security.

He needed only urge his horse forward a few hundred more paces before he was met by the metal outer wall's first security detail. A thirty-something man with blonde hair and blue eyes wearing a dark blue uniform, indicating his role as a patroller—the Malgarian government's primary police and military force—held up a hand to halt him.

"Back again, eh, Cylos?" the man said as Cylos brought his brown and white horse to a halt. He'd made this trip to Perlatum several times a week for the past four years, so it was no surprise most of the patrollers recognized him by now. He was glad to see it was one of the friendlier ones he'd taken a liking to.

"Back here same as you," Cylos began. "You know how it is. A job's a job."

The patroller responded with a smile. "Don't I ever. But I live ten minutes from here, I don't ride in from the middle of nowhere like you do, so it surprises me you keep coming. Anyway, I'll still have to check everything's current. You know, just a formality."

Cylos was already reaching into a pocket of his gray-green trousers to hand over some folded parchments, proof of his current employment in the city. This would allow him much quicker access to bypass the other security checks outside Perlatum—one of the perks of a job in the big city rather than working in the tiny village of Wentsling.

After leaving Fillenglen, Cylos's father had immediately asked him to help contribute financially for his family. If they didn't all do their part, they weren't going to make it. Cylos had felt uneasy about this, uncertain how he could best contribute. But if his father deemed it necessary, he would follow his directive.

He started by working odd jobs in Wentsling, but it didn't take him long to realize they didn't fit his strengths. Besides, if he truly wanted to contribute to his family with his fledgling skillset, he needed to go where there were options for greater earnings. As soon as he was thirteen he took advantage of the better pay and unique opportunities in the city. His mother hated the idea of Cylos traveling so far to work, but she'd since grown accustomed to it. His father had expressed on many occasions how proud he was of Cylos. This was enough for him.

That wasn't to say he loved his line of work, nor that the responsibility, risk, and pressure hadn't occasionally left him terrified, but he'd excelled at it, it provided a good income, and he considered it an improvement over the menial farm and repair work he'd started in Wentsling. Cylos didn't want to let his father down, but that life wasn't for him. At least his work in Perlatum afforded him the chance to get out and see the world.

"Everything looks in order. Go ahead," the patroller said, returning the documentation to Cylos and allowing him to pass through a formerly locked gate rather than wending his way to the next series of checkpoints.

As Cylos continued forward on his horse, he was greeted by the sound of rushing waves on golden sandy shores as he drew closer to his destination at the docks. Perlatum was about as different from Fillenglen as it could get. The crowds, the security, its familiarity across Malgar, and particularly its warm climate were a far cry from the tiny, secluded village where Cylos grew up. At first the sight had shocked him, but he'd grown accustomed to the bustling marketplaces, crowded narrow walkways, palm trees lining the streets, sandy shores, and misty humidity from the sea.

He weaved his way through town, departing from the main buildings and docks where most of the crowds amassed. Slowing his horse, he headed toward two more heavily guarded areas.

The first was secured by more patrollers who, recognizing him, waved him through. The second was protected by four muscular men in short-sleeved tunics and knee-length trousers standing behind a metal gate with pointed spikes at the top. The first several weeks Cylos was on the job, these guards—almost always the same four each time— had routinely scrutinized his credentials, peppering him with questions, skeptical of his right to enter the area. They always eyed the black-and-gold-hilted sword from Belza strapped to his back with great suspicion, nearly refusing to let him enter with it the first few times he'd tried.

Ultimately, he'd convinced them it was necessary for the job. He'd never once seen any of them crack a smile, and based on their continued presence guarding the gate despite their assortment of scars, crooked noses, and battered eyes, he shuddered to think what those they'd fought with looked like afterward.

Fortunately, they too had come to recognize Cylos. So, while they tended to spend much more time checking his documentation than any of the patrollers, they no longer bothered him as they once did.

"Morning," the tallest of the four brutes grunted. "Your credentials?"

"Of course." Cylos never knew whether to smile and act friendly around them or if they'd respect him more if he matched their stoicism. He landed somewhere in between, giving a thin, toothless grin but keeping his eyes narrow as he handed over his paperwork.

Two of the men scrutinized the papers while the other two stood alert, eyes fixed on Cylos. There wasn't much to read and nothing had changed with the certifications for months, so he wondered every time what took them so long. Perhaps they frequently faced counterfeiters with falsified documents trying to sneak in, or maybe any failure came with harsh punishment they weren't willing to risk. Cylos wasn't sure, but he was always surprised by their meticulousness.

"You're clear to pass," the man said after a while. "Remember, the sword stays in the sheath. You may need it for the job, but there's nothing you'll need it for in this area. And don't forget, you are autho-rized for the main path leading to the furthest northern dock only. No deviating from it. Understood?"

They reminded him of these same details almost verbatim every time so of course he understood. But rather than voice those thoughts, he responded with a curt nod and, "Yessir." Then they returned his docu-mentation. Cylos had no interest in causing trouble with these grunts, so he'd never once considered disobeying their instructions.

Cylos didn't know what else lay within the gated area they protected and he'd never felt inclined to ask. As long as he could perform what he needed to unbothered, he wasn't going to make a fuss.

His horse moved forward at a slow walk on the indicated descending path for a few more minutes until he saw a familiar band of misfits. Three men and two women came into sight, sitting in a circle on his assigned dock, waiting for a ship to come in.

The tallest of the bunch saw him approaching and stood up to greet him as Cylos dismounted his horse and tied it to a wooden pole at the end of the dock next to the others' mounts. "Ah, there you are. Every day I wonder if you might quit showing up, but you never let me down. Glad you made it, my boy. We should be in for a busy day."

The man who spoke was Cylos's boss, the employer and organizer of their small crew, Krinton Belweather.

He was in his forties with a black beard and greasy hair. He seemed to never wear clothes that fit him right, perhaps because his proportions were so odd. He had a potbelly on top of long chicken legs and a wide torso that made his neck seem almost nonexistent. Cylos felt he was always smiling, which suited his personality but did his appearance no favors due to his worn down and crooked teeth. Cylos couldn't fathom how someone as rough around the edges as Krinton had made the necessary connections to oversee their operation in such a well-protected location, but he'd never asked. He'd decided it was better not knowing.

For the most part, Cylos didn't mind Krinton. He was rather odd and obnoxious, but he'd given Cylos a chance from a young age when he was first seeking work in Perlatum. At the very least he treated Cylos fairly and had come to respect his skills. In fact, Cylos always sensed he was Krinton's favorite of the group.

Cylos could tolerate Krinton's personality quirks and outspokenness. It was his political viewpoints he struggled with.

"As I was saying," Krinton began, returning to a conversation he must have held with the other four before Cylos arrived. "The new prime minister, Malvus Lorenzus, did you hear what he plans to do? Apparently, he's pushing to reinstate shadow casting. Setting up a new government arm called the Legion of Shadow Casters. Or 'LoSC' as he calls it. More like '*Lost*' if you ask me, eh?" Krinton let out a loud guffaw at his own joke, sending spit flying from his mouth. The others joined in, albeit half-heartedly.

Cylos had heard a lot about Malvus Lorenzus. What little he knew, he greatly admired. The man had staked his entire political career on legalizing casting. And after all the hardship Malgar had endured since the start of the Purge, certainly during Cylos's entire life, public sentiment appeared to be shifting in Lorenzus's favor. People were eager for change and improved lives.

But not all people, apparently, if Krinton Belweather's shameless stance was to be believed. Although Krinton's words had been spoken in opposition, his mere statement hinting at shadow caster reinstatement sent excited chills up Cylos's spine.

"You're awfully quiet about it, Cylos," Krinton blurted in his obnoxious tone, probably noticing Cylos was the only one who didn't force a laugh. "What do you make of it?"

A distant memory touched Cylos's mind—his father denying knowledge of Belza's true identity in the face of the brigands threatening the village and Belza saying his bluff was justified to keep him and others safe, even though Cylos had originally considered it cowardice.

Sometimes he still felt the latter, although he was now guilty of the same.

"Well, I'd say the prime minister has his work cut out for him, wouldn't you? A lot of people won't take too kindly to the changes." Cylos was desperate to advance the cause of shadow casters, advocate for them, help them, bring them safely out of hiding. And yet, here he was playing along with their detractors, just to be safe. He'd tried to come across vague to not betray his true feelings, but he recognized full well how his words would be interpreted by the others.

It frankly made him sick.

But as determined as he'd been—as he still was—to stand up and do all in his power to advocate for casters, he found himself at a loss of where to start. Casters were all in hiding. What could he do? How was *he* supposed to help?

Outside of a few brave politicians like Malvus Lorenzus and others in heightened positions, most common people who backed casters were too scared to speak out while their abilities were yet illegal. Cylos counted himself among them. It was still dangerous to express support for casters. How would he know if his declarations of advocacy would be meaningful or would fall on deaf and threatening ears? He didn't see a feasible way to live up to his commitment. In the five years since leaving Fillenglen, as far as Cylos knew, he'd never even met another caster. As much as he yearned to do something, he found himself unsure how he could help as deeply as he wanted.

If the newly elected prime minister had his way, the opportunity could soon arise. Perhaps there would no longer be a reason to keep support for casters secret. Maybe casters and their proponents could come out of hiding for good and Cylos would finally find his calling and purpose.

But for now, he had to continue to be discreet. To do his part to provide for his family, to keep them safe by being prudent and patient. He couldn't risk losing his employment or endangering himself or his family by speaking out without a sound strategy. Unfortunately, this required he try to find his place in a world that didn't feel like home amongst lonrelmians, many of whom he didn't feel were his kin. It was little wonder constant thoughts of Belza stuck with him over the years.

"I'd say your comment is an understatement," said Victor Hadley, a dark-haired, tan-skinned teenager. "The prime minister may have some backing in central Malgar, but he'll be lucky to find support across the Plate, especially on the outskirts."

Victor was seventeen like Cylos, and, though Cylos didn't consider himself close with any of Krinton's crew, Victor was easily Cylos's favorite. Krinton had only brought him on a few months ago, but he and Cylos had taken an instant liking to each other, albeit in limited interactions. Perhaps it was only because they were close in age and the youngest of the group, but Cylos enjoyed Victor's company more than anyone else's and found himself wishing they could spend time together as friends rather than limited interactions as fellow employees.

The other three of the group—Yezlita and Sharlee, two rugged, brawny middle-aged women, and Darlos, a tall, lanky man in his fifties —mumbled or groaned non-committal responses as well, indicating they either didn't care or it wasn't something they wanted to discuss with the obstinate Krinton. Their boss either didn't notice or was too flippant to care as he moved on from the subject with all five of his subordinates now assembled.

"Anyway, like I said, we've got a big day today." He paused, smiling at them and rubbing his hands together, like a little boy who'd overheard something from an adult he wasn't supposed to know about. "Remember the package I told you about a couple weeks ago? The big one? Well... it should arrive today."

CHAPTER 10

AN ANTICIPATED SHIPMENT

Cylos and Victor both let out a slight gasp at Krinton's declaration. The three others, who had looked completely disinterested before, perked up with wide eyes as all five put their full attention on their boss.

Dozens of shipments came into Perlatum every day. As Malgar's largest port city, Perlatum received boats carrying goods from across the Great Malgarian Plate, particularly Far South Malgar, and from the smaller Malgarian islands dotting Tseloria's surface. But the shipments to Krinton's dock were unlike any others. The boats delivering to him bore goods carrying a heavy price tag. Their senders or their receivers, or perhaps both, paid an extra price to ensure their packages arrived safely.

That's where Cylos and the other members of the crew came in to earn their keep, as couriers of the high-priced goods and packages.

Most of the risk was on the sailors bringing the goods into Perlatum. Out alone at sea, their vessels tended to be the most vulnerable to pirates or other ne'er-do-wells, so Cylos couldn't imagine what they were paid. Typically, if the high-priority goods made it into port, there was little risk of interception from there. Cylos's courier team was tasked with performing the final delivery, and usually they went undisturbed, especially if the package was being sent somewhere as simple as nearby in Perlatum.

But there were always those rare instances when someone shady found out about a valuable package, or a delivery to a different town where the risk of theft or attack became higher. Cylos had faced a few unnerving situations while delivering these high-priced items for heavy spenders, but he'd always come out fine. A previous colleague—the one Victor Hadley had replaced on their team a few months back—hadn't been so lucky. It could be dangerous work, but that was why it paid well.

The furthest Cylos had ever traveled to make a delivery was a three-day journey. His parents had been worried sick, but he ironically hadn't run into any threats. He'd actually found the trip exhilarating. He hadn't been anticipating such a journey today, but if the package promising the massive payout Krinton had told them about two weeks before was coming in, and if Cylos was fortunate enough to get assigned said delivery, he imagined he could be in for a trek. In theory, it would be well worth it.

To Cylos's knowledge, there wasn't necessarily anything nefarious taking place with their deliveries. They were merely compensated by wealthy people willing to pay a premium to ensure items they deemed of great importance were delivered safely and discreetly to the right hands. At least that's what Cylos convinced himself to justify the confidential courier work he'd become an expert at, even when delivery details were sparse or when threatened by scoundrels. Then again, he rarely saw the goods he delivered and Krinton was constantly reminding them, *"We never ask questions. We finish our job."* So perhaps Cylos should have been more wary, but he did his best to shrug it off.

Cylos didn't think it possible for Krinton's smile to grow any wider, but he was proven wrong. The grimy man looked like he might break out in a delighted giggle by how captivated they all were at his announcement.

He looked over his shoulder before turning back to them. "Ah, and what do you know, there's the ship coming in now. Let's go meet them and see what they've got for us."

Cylos looked up. Sure enough, a tall metal barge with a single sail in the middle was headed their way. Each member of Krinton's crew followed behind their boss as he walked down the dock toward the incoming boat. Cylos was as eager as any of them but tried his best to hide it. Yezlita, Sharlee, and Darlos, meanwhile, followed Krinton so closely it reminded him of a trio of spoiled dogs tailing a master they knew held a treat in his fist.

As they advanced, Victor hung back with Cylos and whispered, "What do you think it is? And more importantly, who do you think Krinton will give the big job to?"

Like all of them, Cylos hoped he'd be the one picked. Krinton had been telling them about this delivery for two weeks now. He claimed to have caught wind of it heading their way and said if the task was completed, it would net the deliverer an incredible payout, over ten times more than any Cylos had received to date.

His heart raced as he thought about what he could treat his parents to with the money and how proud they'd be of him. Perhaps they could upgrade their little wooden hut or move somewhere with more land outside of Wentsling, closer to Perlatum. He'd love to take pressure off his father who always seemed one bad harvest away from desperation. Cylos might even reward himself with a couple weeks off if everything went his way. Maybe he could use the spare time to take a trip to central Malgar, where most of the work to restore casting was allegedly taking place, to see if he could make any connections or find a way to help. The thought took his breath away.

But he decided to play it coy with Victor.

"No clue what it could be. And as much as I hope you or I get the job, my bet is he gives it to old Darlos. He's worked for Krinton the longest."

"Yeah, but he's flubbed a lot of operations lately. He's getting slow. If this delivery's set to pay as much as he says, I bet Krinton will pick someone he can rely on better."

"Alright, you all wait here," Krinton interrupted as they came to a stop at the end of the dock and the large metal barge approached. Cylos was relieved he'd been spared the need to reply to Victor. "I'll go up and talk to them."

"Just you?" Darlos asked with disappointment in his voice.

Krinton met his gaze with a wide smile. "Just me. I need to confirm a few things. Don't you worry, though, I'll be right back." As soon as the side of the boat was in reach, Krinton stretched out a hand to grab the ladder on the side and scurried up. Darlos, Yezlita, and Sharlee hung their heads as their boss disappeared from view over the side. Cylos was surprised when the two women then turned toward Victor and him with venom in their eyes.

"You little runts better pray Krinton doesn't choose either of you for the big delivery. If he does, watch your backs. It's not about who starts the job, it's who finishes it," Yezlita threatened with a sneer, her yellowed teeth showing beneath an unkempt black ponytail pulling her forehead back tightly.

Cylos took a half step back and raised his eyebrows. The two women were cold on a good day, but this nevertheless felt out of character. To his surprise, Victor didn't seem fazed and merely chuckled. "Oh, I'll watch mine alright, but just to keep track of how much distance I put between us. You couldn't dream of keeping up with me."

Sharlee's dark eyes narrowed as she took a step toward Victor, staring him down as she pushed a strand of frizzy brown hair behind one ear. "Big talk for a newbie, and a young one at that. We've tracked down and bested targets far more skilled than you, little boy. Trust me."

Yezlita put a calloused hand on Sharlee's broad shoulder to pull her back. "Eh, don't let his cockiness rattle you," she said to her comrade before turning toward Victor. "It's irrelevant anyway. You've only been here a few months. Krinton would never pick you." She punctuated her point by spitting on the dock between them.

Cylos was repulsed but Victor remained unbothered. He let his eyebrows bounce twice. "You might be right," he said with a shrug. "But rumor has it, what matters is who *finishes* the job." He threw Yezlita a wry smile and wink, which caused the veins on her thick neck to bulge as if her head might explode.

"Hush, idiots," Darlos said, interrupting any rebuttal. "He's coming back."

As Krinton shuffled down the ladder, Cylos heard him chuckling.

"Well, well," their boss began before finishing his descent. "I *do* love when things work out so nicely. Whoever says fate doesn't exist is a fool, I tell you," he concluded as he stepped off the ladder and onto the dock.

"Go ahead. Bring her forward," Krinton hollered to a crewman above as he waved his hand toward shore.

Cylos and the others looked at Krinton with wide eyes. The anticipation was palpable, as was their confusion at his inexplicable statement. Again, he seemed to relish their captivated attention as he drew out the silence by standing and smiling at them with his arms crossed.

He let out another chuckle, then spoke. "I was right. The package is here. And the payment is even better than I expected." He paused for dramatic emphasis, then said with an open palm held up, "Five platinum coins."

Cylos's jaw dropped. He'd never seen a single platinum coin, let alone five. His payments normally came in steel or bronze coins, maybe brass or silver if he was lucky to land a big job. He figured this one would come with a hefty sum of gold coins. Such a large reward was completely unexpected. More so when considering they all knew full well Krinton took a healthy margin off the top for himself.

"I know what you're all thinking," Krinton said. "Just shut up already and tell us who gets the job then, huh?"

Yezlita let out an irritated sigh while Darlos nodded his head rapidly.

"Well, I've been debating back and forth ever since I learned about this package and I think we'll all agree there's only one fair way to select who gets it."

Cylos noted Darlos straighten, his shoulders going back and his head perking up. A touch of an expectant grin touched at the corners of his lips. He was the oldest, most seasoned, and had worked for Krinton the longest. It would be fair if he was chosen.

But Krinton's outburst of laughter made it evident his rationale wasn't about to be the most expected one. "And that's where the fate I talked about earlier comes in. Turns out, including the big delivery, they have exactly ten packages for us to turn in today. So, looks like by good fortune, my decision was made for me."

Cylos cocked his head to one side. He wasn't catching on.

Krinton continued. "For those of you not great at math"—he threw a wink at Sharlee that she either didn't catch on to or chose to ignore— "that's two deliveries apiece. So, to decide who gets the big one, here's what we'll do. You'll each get assigned a first delivery at random, and whichever of you drops it off—with an official stamp of approval, mind you, no cheating!—then is the first back here to the dock will earn the privilege of the lucrative job. And, hey, if you're not the first one back, there's still a second package for all of you today, so you should be grateful for the extra work and pay regardless, eh? Fate, like I said."

Cylos exhaled quietly, trying to keep calm. So it would come down to a competition then. He was oddly okay with that. He'd become Krinton's most reliable runner despite his relative inexperience. He was crafty and quick both with his horse and on foot. Even when the directions to the items' destinations were difficult to decipher, Cylos tended to work it out with little trouble.

He would pit his chances of making the initial delivery and returning to the dock first for the coveted package against any of theirs.

He had expected complaints from the other four, but the only one who showed any disappointment was Darlos, who had assumed the task would be handed to him. Cylos realized he shouldn't have been surprised. Yezlita, Sharlee, and Victor were a confident bunch, and they'd be extra motivated. Winning wouldn't be easy.

"With that arranged," Krinton said, "follow me to the end of the dock. As soon as the first five packages are unloaded and assigned, I'll let each of you get started." Then he added in a sing-songy tone, "Good luck!"

CHAPTER 11

THE COURIERS' SPRINT

Krinton was true to his word and refused to let anyone leave the dock until all five had their packages in hand, claiming he'd disqualify anyone who left early. This meant Darlos, who received the first package off the barge, was left dancing with anticipation after he took hold of a medium-sized crate and unfolded an attached parchment with its delivery instructions. Cylos studied him as he read it, but the lanky man remained expressionless, providing no indication of whether he was pleased with the drop-off point or not.

The destination could be as close as a neighboring area of Perlatum or as far as a different town further inland. In no way would it be a fair competition. Many variables came down to luck such as the required destination and the size of the package. Cylos had to stifle a chuckle at the sight of Sharlee's eyes widening like saucers when she saw Krinton straining to bring her a large sackcloth filled with who knew what heavy items. When she unfolded the manifest with the delivery instructions, she rolled her eyes, unable to hide her frustration with its destination as well.

Victor's and Yezlita's packages were much smaller. Each could fit in their hands, and both remained discreet when they looked at the attached parchments. Cylos was the last to receive his package, and as

Krinton went back to retrieve it from the sailors, Cylos couldn't stop his knees from trembling.

"Alright, Cylos, here's the last one of the first set." As Krinton handed over the wooden crate that fit easily in his two arms below his chin, Cylos could detect something moving within. This made him uneasy, but he tried to ignore the squirming feeling under his skin. The box appeared sealed tight, and he figured it would be out of his hands soon enough. He hoped for better fortune as he unfolded the paper manifest accompanying the package, which would reveal how far he'd need to travel to deliver it.

As he began reading, he committed to playing it coy no matter what was listed. It ended up taking every bit of restraint he had not to react, though, as he felt his heart leap in his chest. His destination was specifically detailed, leaving nothing to chance, and even better it was unbelievably close. Not only was it right there in Perlatum; it was inside the same final gated area he'd passed through before meeting Krinton and the others.

This revelation was astounding. There was no reason he couldn't get there and back to the dock in a matter of minutes. Despite having no knowledge of where the others were being sent, Cylos couldn't imagine any of them receiving a closer assignment. He'd never seen one this nearby in his years as a courier. How had he been so fortunate?

But what about the guards? They had always threatened against deviating off his permitted path. It was a risk. It could slow him down. But he had a work-related reason to do it, and an address he'd been requested to arrive at as proof. Surely if they saw him and gave him any trouble, he could talk his way around it?

"Alright, seems to me you've all had plenty of time to soak in your assignment," Krinton said, interrupting his thoughts. "I expect you all to play fair now. Go!" he shouted.

Cylos was by far the slowest to react, remaining rooted to the spot well after Krinton's command. Staring at his manifest, he remained astounded at the convenience of his destination. This let the four others get a jump on him, including Sharlee despite dealing with her cumbersome bundle. She was the fourth one to reach her horse, but once she strapped the large load to it, she was off right behind Darlos who wasn't far behind Victor and Yezlita who were neck and neck in the front as they charged up the path.

Oddly, Cylos was glad to be the last to reach his horse. As the trailer, perhaps they wouldn't notice him never exiting the gate when the others were sure to pass through on the way to their various assigned regions. He even took extra time and care attaching the crate to the back of the saddle. The horse must have also detected something alive inside as she let out a disconcerted whinny, but Cylos managed to calm her down and finish securing his load.

By the time he got aboard his mount, he was a good thirty meters behind Sharlee and could no longer see the other three.

"Get a move on, Cylos! Why are you going so slow?" Krinton yelled. Cylos thought he picked up on uncharacteristic concern in the man's voice.

But given the stakes and the circumstances, he could see why Krinton would be surprised at his slow start. Still, Cylos wasn't worried. Without bothering to acknowledge Krinton's question, he urged his horse onward at full speed up the path.

As it curved upward and to the left, Cylos caught a final glance of Sharlee's horse before it disappeared from sight. She'd soon be through the gate herself and well on her way to her destination. With any luck, she'd be so focused on where she was headed, she wouldn't notice he was no longer behind her. A small, cobblestone path shot off to the right, and Cylos urged his horse down it, pleased to find the guards at the gate above were never in his line of sight.

With the manifest clutched in his hand, Cylos checked the directions one last time to make sure he'd read them right and confirm he was on the right track. The cobblestone path led to a group of houses tightly packed together. Cylos had seen them from a distance before but had never taken this path to view them up close. Most of them looked lavish and inviting. It made sense why they'd be in a section of Perlatum so secluded and protected. Backing to a pristine sandy beach, these had to be vacation homes for the wealthy.

But the one he sought stood out like a blight from the others. All the windows were dark and covered. A black fence surrounded its exterior. Rather than adorning paint, it was covered in bare wooden planks.

There was no décor, no plants, nothing the least bit welcoming surrounding it. It looked like whoever inhabited it wanted complete and total privacy. Cylos wondered if he might be the first visitor the house had ever received.

But he had no time to waste, so he refrained from further observations. Dismounting his horse, he removed the crate from behind the saddle and approached the gate outside the front entrance. Dangling outside was a rope attached to a bell. He pulled it twice to announce his presence. To his surprise, after a few seconds he heard a loud clicking sound and the gate swung open inwardly, as if some mechanism had been activated from inside the house. Holding the crate to his side, he felt more movement within and a shudder went up his spine. But he shook it off, eager to get the delivery over with and be on his way.

Entering the gate, he walked forward to the black front door. He wondered if he should knock or enter since someone clearly already knew he was there. Before he could decide, the door opened a crack and a voice said, "Ah, good, I've been expecting you. Please, come in and I'll verify and certify your delivery."

Cylos fought the urge to gulp, instead saying, "Thank you," as he pushed the door further open, then stepped inside. He was surprised to find himself in a small, enclosed entryway room providing no view into the house beyond. Even within the front entrance, privacy took priority.

Standing before him was the man who had addressed him and opened the door. If Cylos had felt uneasy or intimidated before, the sight of the person before him increased those feelings tenfold.

He must have been in his forties or fifties. His dark hair was tied up in a topknot, the rest of it hanging about his shoulders. But his face stood out the most. He had a long scar running down it from forehead to chin, crossing over his right eye. The eyelid was also damaged, hanging halfway over his eye, leaving it far more squinted than the other. His face was hard and cold with a piercing gaze.

Forcing himself out of his stupor, Cylos handed the crate to the man. "Here you are, sir. As requested." Cylos hesitated and felt silly about what he was going to say but stated anyway, "I assume you already know but... there seems to be something alive in there."

The scar-faced man let out a chuckle. It was a horrible sound, like metal scraping against metal. "Astute of you. Thank you. But, yes, I'm aware. Would you like to see it?"

Cylos wanted to say no, but for some reason, that wasn't what came out. "I suppose."

The man cracked open the lid and tilted it toward Cylos. He nearly jumped backward in fright when he saw a thick, coiled black snake with a purple stripe down the middle.

The man gave out another amused chuckle, then closed the crate back up. "It's called a Hollen viper. They're native only to a region in northern Malgar called the Hollenglades. Are you familiar with it?" he asked.

Cylos shook his head. "Can't say I am." Then, eager to get going, he extended the parchment with the delivery instructions.

"Ah yes, let me grab the seal to certify the delivery for you."

He took the paper out of Cylos's hands and set the crate on the ground, then opened a drawer in a small cabinet by the inner door and began rummaging around. Cylos had half a mind to tell him to hurry up but thought better of it. This man's presence alone was enough to send shivers up Cylos's spine. He was sure he wasn't someone to be trifled with.

Fortunately, it didn't take long before the man turned around with a metal cylinder in his hand. When he pressed it against the parchment, it left a small red symbol at the bottom of the paper, denoting the package as certified and delivered. Cylos wasn't privy to all the inner workings of Krinton's operation, but every manifest they received was marked with its own specific intricate seal that had to be matched with an identical one by the receiver once the package was in their custody. This ensured each delivery wound up in the designated receiver's hands and the couriers couldn't falsify any deliveries.

The scar-faced man returned the parchment to Cylos, who snatched it out of his hands a little quicker than he'd meant to.

"Thank you for delivering it safely," the man said, appearing not to notice. "That's a lovely blade you carry by the way."

Cylos was taken aback. "Um, thank you... A friend of mine made it for me," he said, though not sure why his nerves had led him to the further elaboration. "Well, I'd best be going. Thank you for certifying the delivery." Then, without awaiting a response, Cylos turned away, hustling back out the way he came.

Increasing his pace to a speed-walk, he climbed aboard his horse. The entire experience had been odd, but it was done. He'd delivered the package and had the necessary stamp of approval. Now he could move on.

Though it felt like he'd been at the recluse's house for ages, he pulled a crude watch out of a tunic pocket and was thrilled to discover only a few minutes had passed. It was time to get back to Krinton at the dock. Time to focus on the most pressing matter—landing the big job and completing it.

A rush of excitement ran through him as he grabbed the horse's reins and urged her up the cobblestone path and back to the main road. Before long, Cylos returned to the end of the dock and was surprised to see Krinton Belweather watching him with his arms crossed, wearing a smug grin.

"Hurry up, Cylos, get over here," he said with unusual urgency. Cylos dismounted and trotted over to Krinton. "Listen, kid. I'm glad you finished your delivery as fast as I expected you to. Don't tell anyone, but I peeked through all the manifests and purposely made sure you'd get one nice and close while the others are out on long jaunts."

Cylos's eyes widened in surprise. "You mean you—"

"Yeah, I rigged it, kid. I didn't want anyone besides you to get this job from the very start, but I needed it to appear unbiased. Can't have the others think I'm playing favorites, you understand? Bad for business."

Cylos got what he was saying but still couldn't believe it.

Krinton went on. "Listen, I don't want to waste too much time, but let me tell you, you're the best I've got. You're the only one of the five with a perfect record, so I'm depending on you. This job is a big one, not just for the payout, but for our reputation. And for landing more high-paying deliveries like this in the future, you understand? We *have* to come through."

Cylos envisioned his parents' amazed expressions and tears of joy when he returned to them with five platinum coins in hand. That was all the motivation he needed. "You can count on me, Krinton. Now get on with it so I can get going. What's the package? Where am I headed?"

Krinton hesitated. "That's the thing. This is unlike any we've had before. I honestly don't know what the true package is. All I have is this." He glanced from side to side, checking his surroundings, then, from under his sleeve, he pulled out a long, silver key with a piece of parchment rolled around it.

"The paper has directions to two locations. The first is where the package currently resides. You need to take this key there and retrieve it, then take the package from there to the second destination. That's where you'll deliver and get it certified. Understood?"

"Understood. Sounds easy enough," Cylos responded. "You really have no idea what it is?"

Krinton shook his head. "Nope, no idea. But remember what I always say. We never ask questions. We finish our job."

Cylos had to fight the urge to roll his eyes. There was his old mantra again.

"Right," Cylos said, not bothering to hide his annoyance. As much as Cylos strove to think of his work as merely a means to make a living, he couldn't dismiss the nagging sense that Krinton wasn't exactly a man of integrity.

Shaking off the thought, he took the key from Krinton and removed the parchment with the instructions. His eyebrows raised at the first detail to catch his eye. It said the package was held outside of a town called Lindon, further inland to the northeast of Perlatum, directly north of Wentsling where the Phetos family resided. It was a long ride, but manageable compared to others Cylos had performed in Krinton's employ. He should be there before nightfall if he hurried. There were further instructions mentioning landmarks on a path to the east of town, first a lightning-struck tree, then a rock formation shaped like a sleeping bear, and several others intended to guide him to where he'd use the key to unlock the package.

But more surprising was from there, his journey would take him to Galga City, much further east. This would be the furthest he'd traveled for his job. According to the instructions, there was a small encampment outside Galga where Cylos would meet the person the delivery was intended for. It all sounded straightforward enough, but it wasn't going to be an easy journey.

"I must warn you about one thing," Krinton said in a hushed tone. "That Victor Hadley has been pestering me about this job every day since I mentioned it to the lot of you. He wants it bad. He even offered to do it for a fraction of the reward, claiming he'd let me keep most of his share. But I tell you what, I'll admit Victor's been good for business since bringing him on, but I don't trust him. I can't begin to imagine how, but something tells me he learned about this delivery weeks ago and he knows more about it than he should. Only reason I can figure why he'd be willing to give up the reward to me is if he's got a deal going with someone else. Don't know what kind of fool he takes me for.

"Anyway, Cylos, I know you've had a few close run-ins before with some valuable packages and came out fine, but this one's different. You need to watch your back and use extra caution the whole way. Something tells me you won't make this delivery without facing resistance."

Cylos put a hand to the black- and gold-streaked sword hilt strapped to his back. He never had the chance to receive training from Belza who forged it, but he'd spent significant time practicing with it and found other teachers where he could. In the few times he'd been forced to use it for defense, he'd fared quite well.

"Appreciate the tip. I'll be alright."

Krinton's uncharacteristic graveness finally melted away, replaced by his familiar crooked-toothed grin. "I sure hope so, Cylos. Because if I see you back here again, we'll both be rich, my boy. Remember, I'm counting on you. Now, we're wasting time. The last thing I want is for any of those other four to return while we're here yapping. Get going."

Cylos nodded recognition, pocketing the key and the parchment as he returned to his horse. Climbing aboard and urging her up the path, he began contemplating the best route.

He hated when long journeys took him away from his parents and home for extended time. While they'd come to expect it now and again, this was certain to be his longest absence yet and he knew his mom and dad would be concerned about him. But he forced those thoughts out of his head. If everything went as planned, it would be well worth it. He'd be back to them in no more than a couple weeks with a reward capable of changing their lives forever.

CHAPTER 12

THE PACKAGE

Cylos was pleasantly surprised when he got out of Perlatum and on the northeastern path toward Lindon without any trouble. He'd felt uneasy tugs of nervousness the whole way out of town. If he'd seen Darlos, Yezlita, Sharlee, or especially Victor as he departed, it would have been awkward at best and confrontational at worst. Krinton's comments also left him uneasy. What if someone knew he carried something valuable? What if they tailed him out of town or hoped to intercept him at his destination?

He forced away the intrusive thoughts. He'd done hundreds of jobs like this. There was no sense getting paranoid now. As he pushed his horse on, he took a moment to contemplate what could be awaiting him under lock and key outside Lindon, and why whoever wanted it delivered would go to these great lengths.

Would it be a chest with some priceless heirloom inside? Perhaps a hidden cavern with a mighty weapon stored within? Cylos thought back to the crate he'd delivered with the viper inside and how disconcerting it'd felt to transport a living animal even such a short distance. Hopefully the next item wasn't some dangerous creature. The thought alone made him cringe.

He spent the rest of the journey imagining what he'd do with the reward money. Perhaps the earnings could support his ambition of advancing the cause of shadow casters he'd committed to with Belza five years ago. There had to be something he could do. Removing the ever-present obligation to work to take care of his family might finally afford him the chance to seek out ways and means to help.

This got him thinking of Belza—how dearly he missed him, and of the three items he'd received from the old caster. Cylos hoped he wouldn't regret carrying them with him in his pack while he was presumably at risk of pursuit by thieves or brigands eager to strip him of the key from Krinton and whatever it held protected. If it came down to it, he'd willingly surrender the key or the package before he gave up anything Belza had entrusted to him.

His swirling thoughts made the hours pass quickly and before he knew it the town of Lindon was visible among the boulder-strewn grasslands in the distance. It had been a smooth journey so far, and he was pleased to find the sun still well above the horizon. A couple hours of daylight remained to find the hidden package. Rather than continue north toward Lindon, he banked right, heading east toward the thick forest of beech, oak, and maple trees. He was eager to hit the rough, forested path within that should lead him to the first landmark listed on the parchment.

As Cylos entered the forest and found the old, worn dirt path heading east away from the town, he passed a few travelers headed toward Lindon on his way. Cylos strove to blend in and not rouse suspicion, though his haste as he pushed his horse through the trees earned him some curious looks. He was eager to leave the marked path but wanted to find the lightning-struck tree marking where he should deviate first.

A few minutes later, he saw it, unmistakably matching the description provided to him. The dead tree was split in two in a V-shape, the tops of both ends burnt to a charred black. Reaching it, he brought his horse to a slow trot and veered off the trail into the woods. Now close attention to his surroundings outweighed the need for speed. Becoming disoriented would set him back far more than slowing his pace.

The clues detailed were obvious at first. The rock formation described in the parchment so closely resembled a sleeping bear that

Cylos couldn't help chuckling when he saw it. There indeed was no better way to characterize it. The instructions then led him south to a patch of bushes with fiery-red blossoms, the next clue. He then turned west and traveled several hundred meters forward before he found a rock distinctly marked with a sharp gash chiseled out of it.

Each step and clue took him deeper into the thick wood until he began to realize he may have been optimistic about the daylight he had left given how dramatically the dense tree cover blocked out the fading light. Under the twilight of dusk, he struggled to find the final landmark —a tree with three cavities high in its trunk filled with bird nests. He was fortunate to be clued off by the hooting of owls. After wandering for several minutes in what felt like disorienting circles, he found it at last.

He pulled out the parchment once more and strained to read it. He had a light-rod and a torch in his pack but didn't want to risk illuminating either unless it became absolutely necessary. The last directive was to head due east of the tree with the cavities, where a clearing in the woods would give way to where his assigned package was locked away.

Cylos felt his heartbeat quicken as reality set in on him. He had nearly reached whatever he was searching for. Any moment now, his feelings of anticipation and curiosity would be fulfilled, and he'd be ready to start planning his journey to Galga to make the final delivery.

So far, everything had been far too straightforward to merit such a grand reward. That must mean whatever he was about to retrieve would be incredibly rare or valuable. Or, he worried, difficult to transport. He was eager to find out.

A few more minutes passed before he reached the round clearing. Thinking he'd have to look for a subtle chest or a well-hidden trapdoor, he was surprised to find an outcropping of rocks a few dozen paces in front of him, several of them lumped together to form a conspicuous cave opening. Dismounting his horse, Cylos approached and entered the dark cavity. After a few steps inside, he discovered what the key was intended for. Built firmly into the rocks on three sides and buried deep into the ground below him was a metal-framed apparatus holding a matching black metal grate. The grate had a large lock on the left side holding it shut and blocking off entry into the cave.

Peering through the grate, Cylos could make out a slight flicker of light beyond where the cave appeared to turn to the right. It didn't look like the cave extended very far, hardly a surprise considering the terrain was forested rather than mountainous. The little rocky outcropping provided an ideal natural hiding spot, an obscure bastion deep in the woods that for most travelers could only be encountered by luck. For those who did somehow come across it, the extra precaution of the sealed metal grate would keep prying hands and eyes out.

Cylos let out one last exhale, then pulled the key from his pocket. Slipping it into the lock, the resulting echoing click pierced the quiet night like a crack of thunder. Cylos peered over his shoulder and fought back a grimace as the sound reverberated in his head. After disengaging the lock, he slid the grate open and stepped inside. Closing it behind him, he was glad to find the lock could also be secured from the inside. Locking it up from within, he ensured no one could follow him without a key.

He walked several paces forward, following the natural curve of the cave and the dim flickering light. Once it banked hard to the right, he saw a larger opening ahead with the unmistakable glow of torchlight within. From his vantage point, he could also see a solid rock wall, indicating the cavern ahead was enclosed, a dead end.

This had to be where the package was stored.

Cylos knew he should be moving with more urgency, but he felt overwhelmed with a gripping sense of anticipation paralyzing his system into a slow creeping advance. When he peeked around the cavern entrance, what would he see? His mind spun with the possibilities.

When he reached it, he peered to his left to find none of his guesses had been anywhere close. Leaning against the cave wall was no weapon, treasure, artifact, or dangerous creature of any kind. Instead, it was two children—a boy and a girl who couldn't be older than nine and four, respectively, their clothes tattered and their skin caked in dirt.

When they peered up at Cylos, their innocent eyes grew wide with helpless fright, as if they'd known someone would come and the arrival would only worsen their fate. Cylos's throat went dry like sandpaper and his heart sank into his stomach. He'd spent years convincing himself nothing nefarious was taking place with Krinton's operation, that it was only lowly grunt work for the wealthy. Whether that had been the case or not prior to now, he'd probably never know for sure. But with this lucrative task, evil-doing had to be at work. There was no other explanation. What could someone possibly want with the delivery of a couple captive children?

He'd been so caught off guard at the initial sight of them he hadn't noticed what kept them secured to the cave wall. Looking down, he saw chains wrapped around their ankles and staked into the ground, but what really caught his eye was their wrists. Each child had a metal, rectangular box locked tightly around each of their open hands, completely concealing them. The tip of each of the four boxes had two hinges above the captives' enclosed fingers, while the back featured a slight opening, barely large enough to fit over their wrists, leaving them no way to pull their hands out.

Cylos had only seen these contraptions a couple of times, and never on a person, but he'd heard all about them in his father's stories from the early days of the Purge. When casters were captured or turned themselves in, they were often taken into custody with this lonrelmian invention placed on each wrist to cover their hands, rendering them unable to cast. The slender metal boxes that came in pairs were called caster gloves.

Seeing the two kids gloved, it all made sense to Cylos. The large payout, the secrecy, the hiding spot. The extreme measures weren't used because they were children.

It was because they were shadow casters.

CHAPTER 13

UNSEEN ENEMY

Cylos watched in silence as the children's wide eyes of dread gradually transformed into tilted heads and squinting stares. It was only then he realized his jaw was hanging open and they'd been staring at each other in silence for several moments. They'd probably expected him to say or do something by now rather than stand there gawking. After rubbing a hand back and forth a couple of times across his eyes and forehead, Cylos addressed them.

"What... what are you doing here?" he asked.

If anything, their confusion deepened as he saw the older boy's upper lip perk up and an eyebrow raise. But the glance only lasted an instant before his eyes turned defiant and he said, "Why should we tell you anything? You're here to take us away, aren't you?"

Cylos hesitated. Technically, yes, that's what he'd been sent to do. A weight settled on his heart. The job. The reward. It could all be his by transporting a couple of kids. He'd spent the whole journey dreaming about his parents' thrilled reactions, the new life they could create with the money. He'd known nothing but hardship, struggle, and poverty. This was his chance at something new and better.

Should he go ahead and do what he'd been tasked with? Maybe there was a perfectly moral and explainable reason these young casters were being delivered elsewhere. Perhaps there was a way he could still go through with the job. He could take them to Galga to find out more, maybe talk to them to see what he could find out. There had to be a way to keep the kids safe but still collect the promised prize, right? He'd swear to use the reward to advance good purposes. He didn't want to let go of what it could do for him, what it could mean for his family and his fate. He'd justified his work for Krinton for years, hiding behind ignorance or naivety all this time, what was once more?

We never ask questions... Krinton's words echoed in Cylos's mind.

No. Stop. Cylos shook his head to clear it. Where were these thoughts coming from?

Regardless of what he'd been assigned or what he could earn, seeing the two casters before him changed everything. They were terrified. He didn't need to ask anything to know they were being held against their will and in captivity to be delivered for nefarious purposes. Taking them to the unknown in Galga would be far too risky. Casters or not, he wasn't about to get tangled up in a plot putting a couple of kids in harm's way. Their identities as shadow casters made the situation more precarious, but it didn't change that he had no intention of following through with Krinton's assignment. No reward was worth that mark on his character and conscience.

He forced away his previous temptations and the thoughts on Krinton's complacency about the motives behind their assignments. If he dwelt on them much longer, they'd make him angry. Cylos felt ashamed for thinking them in the first place. Belza would have been so disappointed. Cylos had been seeking opportunities to make a difference for casters for years. This could finally be his chance. He could never live with himself if he ignored it for a reward of any size. He promised himself he wouldn't.

Intending to reason with the children, he approached them and dropped to one knee so he could speak at their level. They probably thought he was crazy for his prolonged silence and inexplicable head shaking, but he hoped to earn their trust. "Listen, you're right. I was sent here expecting to find an object to deliver. But I was never told it would be a couple of kids. I take it from the gloves you must be casters, right?"

Neither child responded, but their sharp flinches and the sheepish glances they exchanged removed any doubt.

"It's okay, you don't need to be afraid. I'm on your side. I won't hurt you. In fact, let me help you. Tell me how you got here and where you're from."

The girl's shimmering green eyes looked hopeful, and they turned glossy as tears began to form. She opened her mouth to speak but the boy nudged her with an elbow and responded instead, his brow furrowing. "You're only acting nice to us so we won't cause a fuss. We're not telling you anything. Wherever you're taking us, you should know a lot of people out there will want to help us. We won't go quietly. We know they want us alive."

Cylos let out a sigh. All he wanted to do now was help. Although, unable to imagine what the children had been through, he couldn't blame them for being guarded. His mind was reeling. How could he get through to them? Then an idea struck him.

"Let me show you something," he began, unslinging his pack from his shoulder. As he rummaged through it, he said, "First off, my name is Cylos. Will you tell me your names?"

The little girl looked to the older boy who kept his mouth sealed shut in a scowl.

"Alright, when you're ready," Cylos continued, keeping his voice calm. He found what he'd been looking for and pulled it out of his pack. "One of my closest friends was a shadow caster. His name was Belza. Before he died, he entrusted this book to me. Look." He held the book in their direction and thumbed through the pages. "You see this? He jotted down his shadow casts and asked me to keep this safe for him. I've kept it close at hand ever since."

"How did he die?" the girl asked. Her voice was more curious than sad. Cylos looked into her eyes and felt his chest tighten. Such a somber question from one so young.

"He died defending my home village, Fillenglen. He gave his life making sure not a single person in the town got hurt, even those who were against casters. At that moment, I swore I'd stand up for shadow casters the rest of my life. I haven't actually met one since then to provide me the chance... But I have that chance now."

A rush of guilt swept through Cylos. He claimed he'd sworn to stand up for them, but had he lived up to that commitment? Had he done enough? Had he done *anything*? Moments before he'd contemplated sticking with the job for some money. Was he being an impostor?

No, a moment of silent weakness didn't change his true convictions and desires. Cylos looked straight in the defiant boy's eyes. "And I'm not going to squander it. I promise you, I will help you. You just need to tell me how."

The boy's features softened and Cylos thought he'd gotten through to him, but soon his eyes narrowed in renewed skepticism. "How do we know you didn't make that story up? Maybe you stole the book from a caster you killed? Sounds like something a lonrelmian might do."

Cylos could have taken offense at the comment, but he brushed it off instead. The boy was understandably jaded and Cylos acknowledged that in many cases, his statement could ring true.

Cylos turned to the next page in the book to reveal a drawing of an alcier. A smile crossed his face. "See this alcier? It was one of Belza's favorites. He even let me ride it. Such a majestic and powerful creature, yet gentle. I'll never forget the feeling of the soft fur on its strong neck and the warm dampness of its muzzle. The alcier was one of the casts Belza used to defend my village. I'll never forget it."

He put all the sincerity he could into his declaration, resulting in a silence hanging over them. It was finally broken by the young girl. "Zane, I think he's telling the truth," she said. "I think he can help us."

At first he threw her an angry glance, no doubt for saying his name, but he didn't offer an argument. As he turned back to face forward and bit his lower lip as if searching for words, another thought struck Cylos.

"Here," he said, reaching into his pocket and pulling out the parchment he'd received from Krinton. "I won't hide anything from you. This is how I found you. I was given a job to locate you. I'll only be paid if I take you to Galga City. Read it for yourself."

The boy's eyes grew wide. "Galga? No, you can't take us there," he exclaimed.

"I won't," Cylos responded immediately, his palms open to calm the boy. "That's what I'm trying to tell you. If I were here to harm you or turn you in, Galga would be my destination. I assure you, I won't take you there. But it will be dangerous traveling with two casters aboard my horse with me. It will be cramped, we'll have to go slow, and we'll need to avoid main roads. But I will do whatever it takes. You just have to tell me where to take you."

The two children looked at one another as if trying to communicate with their thoughts.

"Go on, Zane. Tell him," the girl insisted.

"You realize this could all be a trap, right? Maybe he gets paid more if we lead him and his allies somewhere else."

Frustration rose in Cylos's chest, amplified by having no idea how long they'd be safe lingering here, or if others could be in pursuit while they spoke. But he strove to remain calm. "I understand why you're scared. But you have my word that I'll keep you safe and get you away from whoever has done this to you or wanted you taken elsewhere. Tell me what you can and where we can go to be safe."

Zane let out a deep sigh. Cylos could tell he was unsure if what he was about to say was best, but the boy let it out anyway. "Look, we don't understand everything going on. If you're tricking us, then you already know more than we do. But our parents are shadow casters who have been helping lots of casters remain hidden. With the rumors that casting will be legalized, they've started meeting with other hidden casters and a few trusted lonrelmians. But someone either found out or betrayed us. Some bad men captured my sister and me while my parents were away. Now they're planning to hold us ransom to get our parents to reveal where other casters are hiding.

"Whatever they're hoping to accomplish, it won't work. The new prime minister is bringing casting back. Enough people are tired of all the chaos and crime in Malgar. But they seem to think they can take one last swipe at casters before then. That's why they want us.

"I don't know who they are or why they brought us here. All we heard was it would be too dangerous and risky for them to take us the rest of the way. This was as far as they dared go with us. They said they needed a professional. We figured that's why you came. You seem too young to be a professional though."

Cylos stopped himself from rolling his eyes, but he did lower his chin and raise an eyebrow at the boy.

"A-anyway," Zane continued, "I overheard them saying word was sent out across Malgar guiding people here to complete the task of delivering us to their boss. Something about whoever could prove they were the fastest would get the reward or something like that."

At these words, Cylos felt his blood turn cold. If word was sent out across Malgar, that meant Krinton wasn't the only one informed about the job and the secret location. Cylos liked his odds against any member of Krinton's crew if they somehow caught up to him, but if word had reached other corners of Malgar, then people far more skilled and dangerous could be headed his way any moment. He hoped his fortune as the first to arrive was evidence that Krinton had received directions before anybody else, or at least that the others were coming from further away.

"We need to go now," Cylos said, and the two siblings flinched backward at the urgency in his tone. He pulled out the same key he'd used to open the grate at the cave entrance. "I assume this will work for your chains and the gloves," Cylos said.

Zane shook his head. "For the chains, probably, so you can get us out of here. But only our captors and those waiting for us have the special key for the gloves. We're stuck in these." He frowned and lowered his head.

"Don't worry, as soon as you're safe, we'll figure out a way to get them off. I promise." He flashed him a smile in an attempt at cheering him up. Then he set to unlocking their chains. As he worked, he turned to the little girl. "So, I gather your brother's name is Zane, but what's yours?"

A tiny smile spread across her face. "I'm Maya. Maya Montegue."

"It's very nice to meet you, Maya," Cylos said, returning the smile.

"And I'm Zane Montegue," her older brother declared, as if eager to solidify the introduction.

"Nice to meet you, too. Zane." Cylos sensed they were starting to trust him. He was glad, but at the thought of the kind of malcontents heading his way, he suddenly felt an overwhelming sense of dread. Was he in over his head? He hoped their newfound trust in him wouldn't be short-lived.

Once they were both unchained, he helped them to their feet one at a time, grabbing beneath their shoulders since they couldn't give him their hands while trapped inside the metal boxes. He took a moment to observe the hinged caster glove on Zane's right wrist, curious if there was any way he could break it open. The slender rectangular metal box encasing Zane's open hand within was sealed tight. Cylos stepped behind Zane to get a better look at the back end against his wrist where the two locks were located.

On either side of the opening surrounding Zane's wrist on the inside of the pair of locks, there were two little holes along the inner seam where the gloves would open if unlocked. They provided access to an internal ring mechanism that could expand the opening for larger captives or shrink it to better fit smaller wrists like the children's so they couldn't slip their hands out. But these holes were far too small for his key to enter, as were the pair of locks on either side of them.

The four caster gloves on Zane and Maya's hands were identical and equally secure, so he decided Zane was right and it was futile for now. They were too short on time to further scrutinize the gloves anyway.

"Let's get a move on," Cylos said. "While we walk, tell me where I should take you."

"Are you familiar with Central?" Zane asked, walking beside Cylos.

Cylos shook his head. "I know about the region of central Malgar in the middle of the Plate. Is there somewhere more specific you're referring to?"

Zane lowered his head. "I don't know for sure. It sounds like the old crown city of shadow casters was a town in the middle of Malgar that's long been abandoned. But I think the new prime minister plans to move the capital there and call it Central. I know our parents have been calling it that. But Maya and I have never been there."

"Is there anywhere else safe I could take you?" Cylos asked.

"It seems nowhere is safe these days. Most of our hiding places have been uncovered by anti-casters. I think our best shot to find our parents is to get to Central somehow."

Cylos didn't like the idea of heading somewhere he didn't know how to get to or if it even existed, but he wasn't about to show his doubts in front of the children. "Well, if it used to be a key city for casters, I'm sure it'll show on a map somewhere. We'll be careful and head east away from any main roads until we can find a way there. You two will stand out with caster gloves on, so you may need to stay hidden while I go into an outpost to ask directions or get a map. But trust me, we'll figure it out. Just so long as we steer clear of Galga, right?" he concluded with a smile. Cylos had no intention of making light of the moment, but he thought the reassuring comment would lower the tension.

"Thank you, umm...?" Maya hesitated.

"It's Cylos," he reminded her.

"Oh yeah. Thank you, Cylos," she said, flashing him a smile.

When they reached the grate, Cylos was disappointed to see the forest outside was dark now. He removed the key to unlock it, slid it open, then stepped through first, motioning for the children to follow. Once they were clear of the grate, he slid it closed then locked it up again before pocketing the key.

His loyal horse was visible thanks to the moon and starlight overhead, munching on some grass right where he'd left her. Cylos turned toward Zane and Maya and put his right index finger to his lips, then motioned for them to follow. Arriving at the side of the horse, he gave the steed a reassuring stroke on the back of her neck before lifting Maya into the back of the saddle. He then held out a hand to Zane, who displayed some experience with horses by stepping in the stirrup with one foot. Cylos then took a hold of his left forearm below the caster glove to provide support and Zane swung his other leg over to sit in front of Maya. She threw her arms around his waist as best she could. Cylos couldn't imagine it was comfortable for Zane with the corners of the two metal gloves jabbing into him. But he showed no sign of discomfort toward his sister.

Cylos was about to climb aboard himself to sit in front of Zane when he detected sprinting footsteps rushing right for him.

He clutched the hilt of his sword, unsheathing it with a dramatic whoosh, and turned in a defensive stance toward the approaching steps. His sword was met with a slash from an opposing blade, clanging against his own and sending sparks flying. His body tensed. He hadn't moved a moment too soon.

Zane and Maya gasped in unison and Cylos clicked his tongue twice before flicking the horse in her rear haunches with the back of his offhand. Returning his grip to the sword hilt, he struggled to ward off the push of his attacker's blade. The horse caught on, dashing away to remove the children from the scene. Cylos trusted her to stay close enough so he could call her back.

If he survived, that is.

The attacker removed his blade then swung at Cylos again, aiming for his head this time. Cylos took half a step back, raised his sword in time to parry, and for the first time took in his foe's appearance. He was about Cylos's height and build, but Cylos couldn't make out facial features hidden behind a metal helmet with only a single horizontal slit for his eyes. The attacker swiped at Cylos three more times, powerful swings at ankle, stomach, then neck level. Cylos easily blocked the first two, but his timing was off on the third, sending him off balance as he tipped to the side and stumbled backward.

Recognizing his vulnerability, he wasn't about to attempt anything rash. Instead, he let the momentum of his stumble take him all the way to the ground, using the fall to convert into a dodge. Placing his left hand on the leafy ground for stability, he rolled away from his attacker.

His graceful move was well-timed as his foe stuck his sword into the ground right where Cylos would have landed if his stumble had turned into a clumsy fall. Taking two steps back, Cylos regained his footing to stand in a defensive stance. He began to wonder if the confidence in his swordsmanship was exaggerated. His attacker was skilled and Cylos toyed with the idea of making a run for it. If he could put distance between himself and this attacker then get atop his horse, there was a good chance he could outrun him.

He turned his shoulders to the side to make a break for it through the short grass and into the thicker woods behind when his opponent spoke.

"I always liked you, Cylos. Don't make me hurt you. Call your horse back and hand the kids over to me and I'll let you go. No questions asked."

Cylos couldn't believe it.

"Victor Hadley?" he said, refusing to drop his guard despite the surprise and confusion.

His opponent let out a mocking snigger. "That's right," he replied. "This job is the only reason I got mixed up with Krinton Belweather in the first place. I won't let you stand in my way."

Cylos narrowed his eyes. It appeared his mutual positive feelings for Victor had been misplaced. A surge of defiance shot up his spine through his bones and into the tips of his fingers as he clutched his sword tighter. Glancing at the gold glint of the hilt, his thoughts went to Belza and all the people and children who lived on, including the Phetos family, thanks to his sacrifice.

"That's too bad. Because there's not a chance I'm moving. If you want the kids, you'll have to go through me."

"Have it your way," Victor said, his voice determined. He rushed at Cylos, but rather than standing steady to parry, Cylos dodged, glad his bold declaration had fooled Victor into thinking he would stand his ground.

But though his action betrayed his words, it didn't betray his new motive. He no longer had any intention of running. With Victor over-committing to the swing, Cylos seized his opportunity. The dodge put his sword in an awkward position, but he managed to lash out at Victor's exposed left hip with a swift kick. The missed swing combined with Cylos's strike sent Victor staggering forward. By the time he turned around, Cylos was upon him, taking the offensive with repeated swift strikes of his sword.

Cylos's tactic had worked as hoped, but Victor's skill was undeniable. Despite being forced off balance, he blocked each of Cylos's incoming strikes. At Cylos's fourth slash, Victor met his sword precisely, until both were gridlocked in a match of strength, pressing into each other's swords at chest height with all their might.

As Victor's strength began to prevail and Cylos detected his opponent's sword creeping closer toward him, he kept his composure to take a measured risk. Cylos swiped his sword upward, creating a ringing metallic hiss as the two blades slid across each other, then he immediately sidestepped. Victor's momentum launched him forward, his sword missing Cylos's shoulder by a hair's width, then while Victor couldn't stop his forward progress, Cylos brought a knee up hard into Victor's stomach.

Victor gave out a loud groan, then Cylos brought his sword hilt down on Victor's back before shoving him away. Cylos thought he'd dealt a crippling blow and expected Victor to crumple to his knees next to the tree trunks and rocks at the edge of their clearing-turned-battle-field, but somehow, he kept his balance once again. After rolling over once, Victor popped back up with his sword held high, ready for another offensive. Cylos struggled to hide his disappointment. He thought he'd bested his opponent with the move. He wasn't sure he could do much better.

"Alright," Victor said, frustration ringing through in his voice. "You got a lucky shot in, but I can't afford to waste any more time. This ends here."

As Victor started to charge, Cylos cried out, "Try whatever you want with me. I won't let you harm those children. I'm getting them to safety. I won't let you or anyone else take them to Galga!"

Cylos braced for impact. If Victor's previous fury and skill were any indication, he wouldn't fall for a feint again and would likely batter any parry attempts into submission. Even when Cylos thought he'd gained the advantage, Victor had recovered with little setback.

But the moment Cylos finished talking, Victor skidded to a stop, completely halting his advance, going so far as to relax his sword.

Cylos tilted his head to the side and narrowed his eyes.

"Wait," Victor said, his tone now calm, though carrying an unmissable edge of surprise. "You mean you're not taking them to Galga? You're not going to finish Krinton's job?"

Cylos wasn't sure what to make of this, so he kept his sword held at the ready, merely shaking his head to respond while staying alert.

Victor sheathed his sword in the scabbard at his side then removed his helmet, exposing his dark, unkempt hair and, even in the darkness, Cylos could see the wide grin spread across his face. "Then I think this has all been a big misunderstanding." Victor paused to chuckle then added, "Like I said before, I always liked you, Cylos. Something tells me, we're on the same side."

CHAPTER 14

A CAPABILITY REALIZED

W hat are you talking about?" Cylos asked. "Aren't you here to finish the job and take the reward for yourself?" He was still in disbelief at what Victor had said.

Was it possible he'd hurt Victor more than he was letting on? Was this all an illustrious bluff to salvage his chances at victory by catching Cylos off guard? "Krinton told me you'd been lobbying for the job for days. Even told him you'd do it for less. He thought you were working a deal behind his back."

Victor chuckled, but there was no longer any scorn in his tone. He sounded once again like the friendly boy Cylos had come to know working in Perlatum.

"He told you that? I always knew Krinton had a soft spot for you. Well, I guess in a way he was right. I do have a deal behind his back, but it's not to make money. My only intent is to help the shadow casters."

Cylos's eyes widened at Victor's comment. "You mean, you knew all along this job was to transport shadow casters?"

"Sure did," Victor replied. "A lot of us, casters and lonrelmians alike, have been following this one. Lucky for me Krinton's job was the one to come through. But there could be true enemies eager to collect the reward closing in. Call your horse to get those kids back so we can get moving. We've got a long ride to Central. I can tell you more on the way."

"You mean, you want to do it together?" Cylos asked.

Victor shrugged. "Why not? Sounds like you want to help them to safety too, right? Figure the two of us working together will be better than tackling it alone. You know, a part of me always wondered if you were a caster supporter, Cylos. But it's risky to assume that too hastily these days. I'm glad to know we're on the same side."

Cylos wasn't sure if it was appropriate to consider himself a caster supporter. He hadn't done much to support them. But he kept the thought to himself. Victor was much more informed than Cylos was and, by the sound of things, was already connected with shadow casters coming out of hiding. Maybe this would be Cylos's opportunity to make a difference. He couldn't wait to ask Victor more about it. But for now, he agreed that they'd delayed too long. He hoped they hadn't attracted any attention with the noise from their fight.

Cylos clicked his tongue three more times then whistled. He was overjoyed when his brown and white horse reappeared with the two kids aboard. Their eyes were wide with fright like when he'd first met them, but their expressions changed to confusion when they saw the other boy standing next to him.

"It took a lot to get them to trust me. They might struggle with you as well, especially since you... you know... attacked me and all," Cylos said to Victor as the horse approached.

"Don't worry," Victor replied with his typical bravado. "I've got something that'll help them come around right away."

Victor let out a short whistle of his own and from behind some tree cover, his gray horse appeared with two bags tied to either side of the saddle.

As Cylos's horse came up to him and he nuzzled her head into his hands, Zane looked on in disbelief.

"C-C-Cylos? What's going on? Are you okay? Wasn't he trying to hurt you? We were worried we were... going to be on our own. We almost took off by ourselves with your horse," the young boy said.

Cylos threw him a reassuring smile. "I'm glad you didn't. It turns out there was a misunderstanding." He pointed toward Victor who was rummaging around in one of the sacks attached to his horse. "We know each other. We just didn't know we both had the same intentions. Not to turn you in, but to help you. We're both going to keep you safe together."

Zane's face tightened. "This feels odd. How can we trust either of you?" he asked.

Victor strode over with his hands behind his back. "Zane and Maya, right?" he said with a friendly smile. Zane looked backward over his shoulder, catching his little sister's eyes, then they both nodded hesitantly.

"My name's Victor. I know your parents Adrian and Amelia. They've been looking for you too but asked me to help. They were worried you might be skeptical of me if I found you, so they sent me with something so you'd know you could trust me." He pulled his hands out from behind his back and extended them forward, revealing what he'd been hiding.

Both Zane and Maya's eyes lit up and they gasped. "Our caster beams!" Zane exclaimed.

As Victor held up the circular gray buttons with loose black straps for the siblings to observe, Cylos could barely make out the etchings of the initials "ZM" in one and "MM" in the other. Zane and Maya looked at them with longing eyes. Cylos imagined they wished they could hold them and put them on as he'd seen Belza do years ago.

"Probably best to keep them hidden for now. Do you want me to hold onto them for you?"

Zane bit his lower lip. "I know I can't do anything with it right now, but I'd like mine back if I could. I've got a pocket inside my vest where it will stay hidden. Is that okay?"

Victor shrugged. "I don't see why not." He walked toward Zane, who did his best to indicate where the pocket was despite the metal box covering his hand. Victor reached up, pulled back the vest and, locating the pocket, dropped the caster beam inside. Zane's entire body relaxed as if the beam's presence alone was soothing to him after being separated for so long.

"What about you, Maya?" Victor asked.

The little girl appeared on the verge of tears. "I don't have a good spot for mine. Will you hold it for me?"

"Of course," Victor replied. "Once we get you both somewhere safe, we'll work on getting those gloves off and your beams reattached. We've lingered way too long now. What do you say we get to Central to find your parents?" Victor asked, a confident smile plastered on his face. Cylos envied his unfaltering resolve.

Both children smiled, nodding in response. Victor declared it would be best to balance the weight, so together he and Cylos helped Zane off Cylos's horse and onto Victor's. Then both teenagers climbed aboard their steeds. Cylos looked behind him to see Maya's lower lip sticking out. He knew right away she missed her brother.

"Don't worry, Maya. We'll all stick together. I'll keep you safe, I promise," he said with a smile. Maya exhaled through her nose, then let a smile perk up at the corners of her lips.

"Thank you, Cylos. For keeping us safe," she said. He was glad she remembered his name this time. She put her arms around him to hold on and, as Cylos had expected, it wasn't comfortable to feel the metal edges of the gloves pressing into him, but he wasn't about to complain, especially as she rested her head into his back.

Sitting side by side atop their horses, Victor addressed Cylos. "Stay close by me. We need to stay hidden and I want to get away from this region as fast as we can. We might need to ride through the night. We can regroup when we're well away from here. I'm going to take us the long way to Central. I want to avoid Galga at all costs."

Cylos nodded understanding, then they urged their horses onward. Cylos was exhausted and it sounded like they were in for a long night. But as he felt Maya's steady breathing behind him and the prod of her caster gloves on his waist, he found the strength and determination to press on. He would see to it that both Montegues were delivered safely to their parents, no matter what.

The two horses with their four passengers pressed on well into the night and Cylos was beginning to wonder if they'd ride until dawn. He was relieved when Victor called for a halt.

"There's some shelter up ahead. I don't think we should go any further without food, water, and sleep. We've put enough distance between us and Lindon," Victor said.

The spot Victor had indicated was a rocky outcropping surrounded by dense forest. Tucking themselves into the trees, an overhanging rock and surrounding fallen timber provided shelter. Dismounting their horses, Cylos and Victor then helped Maya and Zane, respectively, off their mounts. Maya had been asleep for at least an hour behind Cylos. After creating a makeshift resting place out of blankets, Cylos gently set her down without disturbing her slumber.

"You get some rest too, Zane," Victor said. "Cylos and I will take turns on watch."

Zane crossed his arms and pursed his lips. "I can keep watch, too. I got some sleep on the horse. I'm fine."

Victor's hands went to his hips and he opened his mouth to talk.

Cylos stepped forward. "You're right, Zane," he interrupted. "You're almost ten years old. You're ready to keep watch. I bet you want to look out for your sister, don't you? How about you sit up against the stump next to her and keep an eye out while Victor and I take care of the horses."

A wide smile spread across Zane's face. "You mean it? You'll let me keep watch?"

Cylos nodded and Zane skipped over to his sister in delight. Victor looked at Cylos with a raised eyebrow, to which Cylos whispered, "Just wait."

Cylos and Victor started tending to their horses and, minutes later, Cylos looked over at Zane to find his head leaning against the stump, his arms and legs limp, as he lay fast asleep.

"Psst, Victor," Cylos whispered, pointing at the young Montegue boy once he had Victor's attention.

Victor looked over at Zane then flashed Cylos a smile. "Well done," he said.

They decided Victor would take the first watch before waking Cylos a few hours later to keep watch until dawn.

As the sun started peeking over the horizon, Cylos was relieved there had been no interruption while the Montegues slept soundly. Roused by the morning light, Victor sat up, stretched and yawned, then stood up to approach Cylos.

"Let's let them sleep a few minutes longer, then we'd better get moving again," he said.

Cylos nodded. "When they're awake, do you think it would be worthwhile to try to get those gloves off them? They can't be comfortable and removing them would make us a lot less conspicuous if we come across any travelers on our way."

"It's a good suggestion. I'd thought the same thing, but I don't know if it's worth it. Those things are designed to be hard to remove for a reason. Without a key, I don't think we have the right tools to get them off. If we tried anything crude, I worry we'd risk hurting the kids. Once we get to Central, we should have no trouble finding someone with a forge who can heat the caster gloves in the right places to destroy the metal and get it off their hands safely."

"Makes sense," Cylos said, but he couldn't hide his disappointment as he lowered his head. He wished there was more they could do for Zane and Maya right then. At least there was solace in knowing he'd rescued them from captivity and was well on his way to getting them to safety.

"Can I ask you something?" Cylos said, curiosity entering his mind as he thought about the siblings. Victor nodded then Cylos continued. "How did you find me last night? And so quickly? I figured you and the others would be too busy with your own deliveries to see me when I left Perlatum. How did you stay so close behind?"

Victor chuckled. "As soon as I received my initial delivery assignment from Krinton and saw it required I go all the way to Yubbitz, south of Perlatum, I knew there was no chance I'd be back first. But it's not like the job meant much to me anyway. I wasn't planning to ever return to work for Krinton after helping the Montegues, so as soon as everyone else was out of sight, all I did was return through the gate to hide where I had a vantage point of the docks. I saw you get back first after your delivery and watched you chat with Krinton, then from there I tailed you as closely as I dared."

"I can't believe I didn't notice. I usually detect when I'm being followed. Either I'm not as good as I thought or you've had a lot of practice," Cylos said.

Victor lifted his eyebrows up and down twice then said with a mischievous grin, "I've got my tricks."

They both shared a laugh and Cylos shook his head. He had so many questions for Victor—about how he'd found out about the job, how he got involved with Krinton, what his work with shadow casters was like, and more. They only had a few minutes of respite before it would be time to wake the Montegues and resume their journey, but he wanted to get as many questions answered as he could.

But as Cylos opened his mouth to speak, Victor's head snapped to the side and his eyes widened as he held his ear up, listening intently. The unspoken words caught in Cylos's throat as he stopped himself to listen. It only took a heartbeat for him to hear what had caught Victor's attention.

"Hoofbeats," Cylos whispered.

"Wake them up now," Victor ordered, his confident lightheartedness replaced with urgency.

Cylos needed no second bidding. Throwing his pack on his shoulder, he scrambled to Maya and Zane's side, rousing them as softly but purposefully as he could. "Maya, Zane, stay calm but we've got to go now," he whispered. "Someone's coming."

Fear filled their faces, but they didn't make a sound. Cylos helped pull both of them to their feet, stuffing the blankets into his pack, then ushered the two children toward the horses. Cylos was planning to help them aboard the mounts when Victor interrupted.

"There's no time," he whispered harshly. "Whoever's coming is nearly on top of us. Go find a place to hide the kids. I'll stay here and stall as long as I can."

Cylos wanted to argue but his resolve faltered. He didn't like the idea of leaving Victor alone but also understood prioritizing the Montegues' safety. So he simply nodded and said, "I'll get them hidden then be ready to back you up."

Victor didn't react, giving Cylos the impression he didn't agree with the declaration. But maybe Cylos was overthinking it and Victor had only felt there wasn't time to risk a response. Regardless, Cylos scooped Maya up in one arm and pressed Zane forward as they tore deeper into the thick trees behind them. Desperately searching for an adequate hiding place, he soon found a hollowed-out log that must have once been a mighty tree.

"Here, crawl inside. I'll be right behind you," he said.

Zane wasted no time, scurrying in on all fours right away, dragging the metal boxes on his hands along the rough ground as he advanced. Maya, however, tightened her grip around Cylos's shoulders and he could feel her forearms flexing as the metal of the caster gloves dug into him.

"Maya, it will be okay, I promise. Please, get inside."

"Cylos, please don't leave us by ourselves," she pleaded, tears forming in her eyes. Cylos felt his chest tighten. He couldn't imagine how much these two had been left alone in fear and uncertainty since their capture.

He glanced down at the log and noticed a small gash out of the center. It appeared large enough to allow him to keep an eye on Victor while they remained hidden.

"I'll go in with you, Maya. But if Victor needs me, I'm going to help him. We won't leave you, though. Everything will be fine, I promise."

The instant the final two words left his mouth, he found himself doubting whether he could keep his word. Depending on who was approaching, he had no idea if he and Victor could hold their own.

But the words seemed to have the desired effect on Maya. She inhaled deeply and her features hardened in an attempt at bravery as she nodded.

"That's my girl," he said. Then, setting her on the ground, she crawled in behind Zane with Cylos bringing up the rear. Maya had closed about half the distance between the entrance and Zane when she yelped, "Ouch!"

"What happened, Maya?" Cylos asked, feeling cramped on all fours inside the hollow log, especially with his pack still strapped to his back.

"I cut my arm," she replied. Cylos peered forward and saw a trickle of blood flowing down her arm and a sharp piece of splintered wood sticking up that she must have scraped against.

"Get to your brother, Maya, then I'll take a look at it." She nodded and continued forward, but Cylos could tell how tense she was from the veins popping on the back of her neck.

No sooner had he and Maya met Zane in the middle of the hollow log than they heard the hoofbeats come to a stop close by. Peering through the slit in the dead tree, Cylos could make out Victor, standing with his sword in a defensive position, as ten mounted newcomers in a variety of armor emerged. Cylos had to suppress a gasp when he immediately recognized the three riders at the front of the group.

"Well, well, look who it is. What was it you said about us never dreaming of keeping up with you?" The jeering voice belonged to Yezlita, bearing a sword atop her black horse. Sharlee was close by with an arrow nocked to her bow and Darlos was off to the side, pointing his spear at Victor. Behind them, seven other riders, four men and three women, stood with weapons drawn as well.

"What do *you* want?" Victor asked.

"What do you think we want?" Sharlee spat. "We're here for the package. The three of us got back to Krinton about the same time and, well"—a wicked smile spread across Sharlee's face—"let's just say we forced the truth out of him. Hope you weren't planning to get your job back. Krinton Belweather won't be running anything out of Perlatum anymore," she concluded with a cruel snigger.

A lump formed in Cylos's throat. He hadn't always seen eye to eye with Krinton, and he had come to realize he probably had no concept of the full depth of the man's seedy entanglements, but that didn't mean he wanted harm to come to him. He'd always treated Cylos well.

Yezlita spoke next. "When we arrived at the locked cave outside Lindon"—she gestured behind her—"we found a few others from other operations with the same task who had already found the cave empty. We got talking and all agreed we wanted a portion of the prize. We told them we had a good idea of who had taken it, so they agreed to join us, and we've been tracking you ever since. We expected to find Cylos at the end of the trail, but I suppose it's no surprise you abandoned your job and joined him. So tell us, where's Cylos and where are the two casters he found?"

Cylos couldn't believe his ears. They knew about the casters? How?

Unless... had Krinton lied and known all along? They said they got the truth out of him. How much had he actually known about the assignment and the package? Or had the others who joined them outside Lindon been the ones to inform them about the casters?

If Victor was as surprised by their knowledge of the situation as Cylos was, he didn't show it. "I have no clue what you're talking about," Victor rebutted.

"Don't play dumb with us," Darlos said. "We're giving you a chance to talk through this and make the smart decision. Either tell us where Cylos is, or we'll brush you aside like we did to Krinton and find him on our own. You think we wouldn't notice both his and your horses right there?" He pointed at the pair of steeds.

Again, Victor didn't show the slightest hesitance despite being obviously caught. "Yeah, I have his horse because I found it abandoned outside the cave at Lindon. Cylos beat us *all* there and was long gone by the time I arrived, so I took the horse for my own. Wasn't going to leave a perfectly good animal behind. Maybe Cylos left the horse to throw pursuers off or maybe he found a better way to deliver the package, whatever it was. Couldn't tell you for sure. But I have no idea where he went, so I'm moving on to something new. You've been tracking me for nothing."

"You really expect us to believe that?" Yezlita asked, her eyes thin.

"You really expect *me* to believe that you all are working together and will share the reward in the end? I'm sure the others only followed you here because you had a lead and you're all working out how to betray each other like you're doing to me now."

All ten riders looked amongst themselves with shifty eyes.

Cylos stifled a chuckle. He admired Victor's stall tactic, turning the questions back on Yezlita and her crew to regain control of the conversation.

"But, yeah, you should believe me. Let me tell you what really happened, beginning back in Perlatum with Krinton," Victor said.

"Cylos, my arm," Maya whispered.

Cylos had been so focused on Victor and the intruders, he'd almost forgotten. He hardly dared to speak and kept as quiet as he could. "Let me see it," he whispered back as he vaguely overheard Victor drag out the conversation with bogus explanations to buy time. Cylos wondered if Victor had a plan or if he was waiting for Cylos to intervene. He hoped to read the situation well enough to contribute in the best way as soon as he'd taken a look at Maya's cut.

Maya rotated her forearm so Cylos could get a good look at it. There was a longer gash than he'd expected—the splintered wood must have been sticking up at the worst possible angle as she crawled and put weight down on her arm right on top of it—but it didn't look serious.

"Try to stay strong, Maya. As soon as we're out of this, we'll get it bandaged up." She looked as though she might cry, but he gave her a reassuring nod, reminding her to be brave and remain quiet. He saw her lower lip quivering, but she nodded in return.

"Cylos... I'm so scared," she said.

Scared.

As Cylos stared into the young girl's damp green eyes, the word struck him with the force of a rockslide. He was scared too. He'd been scared his whole life.

Scared to make the trek and deliveries to Belza. Scared of the bandits threatening his home. Scared to step in and help Belza while he sacrificed himself defending Fillenglen.

Moments before, he'd been too scared to counter Victor's instructions, to stay out and offer his help in the face of this new threat. He'd always been too scared to voice his own thoughts and desires to his father. Too scared to do anything to stand up for casters even after promising Belza he'd dedicate his life to it. For years he'd hidden behind the comfortable excuse of never meeting or knowing a caster.

But the truth was he'd been too scared to act. Too scared to stick out his neck in defense of casters and actively seek a way to help them. He'd been too afraid to ever state his true feelings about casters in front of Krinton and the others, hiding his beliefs out of fear. Zane and Maya had to be thrust in his lap to get him to act. Even then, he'd been tempted to let his fright get in the way again.

Maya could have never guessed how her three-word declaration impacted Cylos, but as he stared back at her trembling face, he felt a rush of conviction unlike any he'd experienced before wash over his body. He'd been scared for far too long.

"I understand, Maya." Cylos kept a firm determination in his tone despite whispering. "Let's be brave together. Soon, you won't need to be scared anymore." He meant it.

Cylos was about to return his focus to Victor and their ten foes so he could size up the situation then follow his conviction with immediate action, when something made him do a double take. Catching sight of Maya's bleeding cut on her wrist below the secured caster glove, his eyes were drawn to the two small holes between the opening for her arm and the locks. Cylos hadn't considered it before, but the distance between the two holes sent a spark of realization through his mind.

If what he thought he'd figured out was right, he had no time to lose.

"Maya, slide back for a second," Cylos whispered as urgently as he dared. He didn't think the others could hear them over their continuous chatter, but he didn't want to risk it. "Zane, I need you to be brave. There's something I want to try on you. If it works, I think we can help Victor. But we need to move fast."

Cylos was pleased when no argument came from either child. They must have sensed the purpose in his tone. Once Maya had scooted to leave enough room, Cylos crawled toward Zane and asked him to hold out his right hand with his forearm facing up. After glancing at the same two little holes on Zane's caster glove that were perfectly aligned with the inner seam and the locks, Cylos delicately unshouldered his pack, desperate to avoid making noise, and he pulled out the tool he'd acquired from Belza, removing it delicately from its small leather sheath.

The two sharp points were extended out in a straight line, pointing away from one another, but Cylos squeezed them toward each other upright until the device let out a click. The sound nearly made him jump in fear of alerting their foes, but Victor and the others were practically shouting at this point, so they hadn't noticed. Cylos needed to hurry. Victor had proven an avid bluffer, but Yezlita, Sharlee, and Darlos were onto him and weren't going to stand around arguing forever.

Holding onto the circular portion of the tool in between the two points that were now spring-locked facing upward, Cylos carefully lined up the sharp ends with the pair of holes on the bottom of the caster glove on Zane's right hand. His hunch thus far had been correct. The tool slid right in.

"Okay, Zane. This tool is from my old caster friend I told you about. I never knew what it was for, but I think I just figured it out. Keep your hand as flat as possible and tilt it back as far as you can. I don't think this will hurt, but I've never done it before, so it might, so please be brave. Do you trust me?"

To Cylos's surprise, Zane didn't even look nervous. Instead, he had a determined fire in his eyes. The sharp spikes of the distinctive tool fitting so perfectly into the holes of the caster glove couldn't be a coincidence.

Zane gave a single nod. "Do it."

As Cylos had done so many times when casually fiddling with Belza's tool, he squeezed the round center as hard as he could. But this time, there was a clear purpose for the force and speed of the tool.

With a loud crack—much louder than the click from before—the spikes of the tool snapped back to their horizontal starting position, slicing through the internal locks of the caster glove, freeing Zane's hand as the metal box swung open on its top two hinges and toppled to the ground where it lay flat with both interior halves exposed.

Though it had gone as Cylos anticipated, he couldn't stop himself from locking eyes with Zane to find they both wore the same wide-eyed, slack-jawed expressions on their faces.

It had actually worked!

But their moment of exhilaration was short-lived when they heard Yezlita yell, "What was that sound?"

CHAPTER 15

REINFORCEMENTS

Cylos had assumed the force of Belza's tool carving through the metal of the caster glove would make a loud sound, but the realization that the noise had exposed them still froze him in a momentary panic. Thankfully, Zane remained more composed.

"Hurry, get the other one off now!" It wasn't a shout, but his voice was no longer quiet as Zane struggled to contain his excitement. Not that subtlety mattered anymore with their cover blown. As Cylos clicked the tool back into place for a second go, Zane reached into his inner tunic pocket with his freed hand and set his caster beam on the bottom of the hollow log. At the same time, Cylos heard Yezlita say, "Keep your weapons on Victor. Don't even think about moving a muscle, boy. I'll go check it out." Then came the sound of trotting footsteps from her approaching horse.

Cylos was more confident after seeing Belza's tool work, so he moved much quicker the second time. He inserted the two sharp points then pressed the circular center to release the spring-loaded spikes. After another loud crack, Zane's second caster glove fell to the ground with another clatter.

"They're in the log!" Yezlita shouted. Cylos's heart skipped a beat and a tingle ran down his spine. With their hiding place spoiled, they were easy targets now. If Cylos crawled back out, Yezlita would pick him off before he could defend himself or mount an attack. They needed a plan and fast.

Zane was well ahead of Cylos. As soon as his second hand was free, he slammed it down against the caster beam button, which ignited and projected a beam of light on the top interior of the log. Placing his hands in the light, he extended two fingers on one hand and a single finger on the other to project a shadowy silhouette on the log surface above him. From out of Zane's shadow symbol projection appeared a jet-black reptile, about a meter long, with a long snout, curly tail, and an armored shell that reminded Cylos of the armadillos he'd sometimes see on his rides to Perlatum. The creature was upside down, its thick claws on all four legs gripping the wood of the log where Zane had projected the shadow symbol.

"Lazzerode, go get her," Zane called, pointing toward Yezlita.

Yezlita gasped. "What the? That light, is that a—"

The shadow cast Zane had called a lazzerode burst through the gap in the wood, sending splinters of the dead tree flying in all directions, silencing Yezlita midsentence. The reptilian lazzerode landed on the side of her horse, invoking a terrified whinny from the mount as it reared back on its hind legs and a cry of dismay from Yezlita. The nimble lazzerode kept its balance with ease, scurrying up the horse's body to leap onto Yezlita's back. Before she could react, the black lizard unleashed a vicious scratch across the back of her neck.

Yezlita let out a shrill scream and reached back over her shoulder, but rather than getting a hold of the shadow creature, she instead lost her balance and toppled off the horse, who sprinted away in fear, abandoning its rider.

Their cover destroyed with the forceful departure of the lazzerode, Cylos remained crouched in disbelief as he took in the scene before him.

Amidst the chaos, Victor charged at Sharlee, cleaving at her bow with his blade to send it tumbling from her hands.

Lacking the proper attire or equipment, Zane crudely strapped his caster beam to the front of his shoulder and ignited it again. Placing his hands in the beam, he projected another shadow symbol from which emerged a dark green and turquoise insectoid, about the same length as the lazzerode but much taller. It reminded Cylos of a mantis with its large buggy eyes, antennae, and creeping legs. But rather than slender, its body was thick and round, and its front legs were covered in sawtooth spikes.

"Cylos, get mine off too!" Maya shrieked, snapping him out of his stupor. He'd been so dazed he hadn't even thought to remove Maya's caster gloves.

As he placed Belza's tool in the holes at the bottom of Maya's gloves, Zane shouted to his bug-like shadow cast, "Mantidus, go help Victor. Lazzerode, get over there, too, he's way outnumbered."

Heeding Zane's orders, the lazzerode abandoned its struggle with Yezlita and scurried toward the other assailants with the mantidus. After disarming Sharlee, Victor had dodged away from the other assailants, taking advantage of their distraction as the pair of shadow creatures headed their way. The lazzerode and mantidus weren't as impressive as the massive animals Belza had summoned and commanded, but they were still spectacular in their own right as wispy tendrils of shadow followed their every movement.

In a matter of seconds, Cylos used Belza's tool to release Maya from her gloved captivity, then stuffed it back into its sheath inside his trouser pocket. With her brother at her side igniting his caster beam to provide Maya with a light, she formed shadowy projections of her own with her hands.

Cylos was eager to see what young Maya would call forth but didn't waste time watching. Instead, calling upon his newfound courage, he dashed for Yezlita and kicked her sword away before she could recover from the lazzerode attack. Unsheathing his sword from his back, he brought the hilt down hard on her head, knocking her out cold.

He then looked up to see how Victor was faring, only to have his breath catch in his throat. At some point Victor had been knocked to the ground. Darlos, Sharlee, and one of the unfamiliar horsemen rode toward him, their weapons trained on the dark-haired boy. The lazzerode and mantidus had provided an initial distraction and were busy giving the other six companions everything they could handle. Still, the newcomers were trained fighters that weren't about to go down easy, even against a pair of shadow beasts, so the other three had returned their focus to Victor.

Victor held his sword above his chest as he scrambled backward. Standing up too fast would put him in easy range of Darlos's spear and the other man's lance, but staying in one spot would convert him into an unmissable target for the hooves of the advancing horses or the throwing knife Sharlee held in one hand, taking the place of her bow. Victor's expression didn't reveal a hint of nervousness, but as the three riders descended on him—Sharlee straight at him and the other two approaching either flank in a pincer movement—there was no way he could ward all three off on his own. He needed help and fast.

The sight of Victor on his back on the overgrown terrain triggered a flash of a memory in Cylos's mind. Belza. Slashed by Thaddeus Ralkentin while Cylos stood back helpless. He tried to rescue him. But couldn't. Belza, lying in the snow, fading. His hand tracing down Cylos's face a final time as it dropped, lifeless. Taken from existence unjustly with so much life left to share.

Cylos tightened his grip on his black- and gold-streaked sword hilt and gritted his teeth. Not this time. He would never again lose a friend while he drew breath and had a chance to intervene.

Storming forward, he let out a guttural yell and was glad when all three foes surrounding Victor flinched in his direction. Their recognition of his advance wouldn't save them. Changing his grip on his sword mid-stride and pulling it back behind his shoulder, he heaved it forward like a javelin, straight for the unfamiliar man nearest him.

It wasn't orthodox, but it was effective. The blade pierced the man through his back while he peered over his shoulder at Cylos. He let out a muffled groan, then looked forward and down at the sword point protruding from his stomach. The man's lance dropped to the ground and he toppled sideways off the horse, landing in a heap.

The distracting offensive gave Victor time to react. He rolled over two times, narrowly dodging Sharlee's thrown knife as it stuck in the ground where he'd been moments prior, then pulled himself to his feet.

Cylos whipped out his dagger and rushed at Sharlee while she scrambled to take hold of a second knife strapped to her saddle. She was faster than Cylos expected, securing a blade and hurling it his direction.

The throw came with deadly accuracy. All Cylos could do in time was raise his dagger to deflect it. The desperate move saved his life, but the size and speed of the throwing knife swept the dagger from his grip with a loud clang as Sharlee's throwing knife ricocheted to the side. His hand stung from the impact of the colliding weapons and where her knife handle struck his knuckles. He'd been fortunate to avoid serious injury.

Sharlee reached for another knife. There was no time to find his dagger.

Cylos sprinted at Sharlee and dropped to the ground in a slide before she could release her throwing knife. Skidding on his back between the horse's front and back legs, Cylos reached into his pocket to pull out Belza's tool. As he shot beneath the horse's belly, he shook it loose of its sheath then stabbed the pointed tool edge into Sharlee's leg, just above the ankle.

She let out a shriek and couldn't stay aboard her mount as she instinctively reached toward her wounded leg. After she'd fallen, her horse sprinted away through the trees.

Cylos had no time to celebrate his crafty move, instead spinning out of the way of Darlos's spearpoint as he stabbed it where Cylos had come to a stop after the slide. Cylos jumped to his feet and dodged backward.

"Cylos," Victor called from his side. Turning his head, he saw Victor had sidestepped toward the brute Cylos felled with the thrown sword and had already removed the blade.

"Catch," Victor said, tossing Cylos's blade back to him.

Cylos snagged the black and gold sword hilt out of the air, then stepped toward Victor. The pair stood shoulder to shoulder, their blades held at the ready.

"Nice of you to show up," Victor said casually. How he could joke and remain so calm at a time like this was beyond Cylos. He nodded at his friend and stifled a scoff by exhaling sharply out his nose while shaking his head, never taking his eyes off their two foes.

Sharlee yanked the pointed tool from her leg and chucked it aside as she growled at the two boys through fuming eyes. Darlos steered his horse next to her, passing her a sword he had strapped to his saddle, opting to keep his spear in hand atop his mount.

"You pathetic kids are finished. One way or another, we're taking the caster brats and getting the reward," Darlos scowled.

Cylos narrowed his eyes and let his nostrils flare. "Not a chance." He and Victor charged. Cylos went straight at Sharlee while Victor advanced toward Darlos and his horse.

Blood streamed from Sharlee's injured leg but whether from adrenaline or sheer force of will, she held her ground undeterred. She glared at Cylos and bared her teeth, ready to receive him.

But nothing would stop Cylos now. He began with a high swipe at her broad shoulders, which she blocked easily, but landing the strike wasn't his intention. She could act unhurt, but Cylos knew the truth. With both their blades held high pressed against each other, Cylos swung his right leg to kick Sharlee's wound with the side of his foot as hard as he could.

She let out a gasping shriek and her whole upper body flinched toward her lower left leg.

It was all the space Cylos needed.

He slashed his sword across her stomach, following it up with a second strike in the opposite direction that knocked Sharlee's sword clean out of her hands before the follow-through sliced a gash across her cheek and upper lip. The impact rotated Sharlee's body sideways as she collapsed to the ground face-first.

Cylos panted as he looked at his blood-stained sword, surprising himself with his own effectiveness. He'd never doubted Belza's craftsmanship, but he was always left in awe at his effortless precision with the blade.

He then turned to find Victor had cut Darlos's spear in half. But the lanky man was resilient and continued to ward him off with the jagged end of the broken spear shaft, using the height of his mounted position to his advantage. He gave a swift kick to his horse's back haunches, preparing to charge forward at Victor to trample him.

Cylos gasped. Would Victor be able to dodge in time?

The horse snorted and sprung off its powerful back legs, but before it could land its first step, Zane's lazzerode leaped from an overhanging tree branch to latch onto Darlos's face, sinking its claws into his cheeks and forehead. The impact startled the horse and knocked Darlos off balance, sending him staggering sideways off his mount. He went down screaming until his voice was abruptly cut off by his head smacking hard against a fallen tree.

With Darlos and Sharlee defeated, Cylos directed his attention to the remaining assailants. Two of the six had already been felled, leaving four still atop their mounts. The lazzerode left the incapacitated Darlos and took advantage of its surroundings once again, scurrying up a tree overhead. It dropped on the shoulders of an unexpecting female rider with sleek golden armor fitted to her muscular arms and shoulders.

While it unleashed bites and scratches on the foe's neck and back, the mantidus came over and knocked the woman off her mount with its sawtooth forelegs before finishing her off with a hard stomp.

Another intruder dressed in black assassin's garb managed to hit the mantidus with a pair of arrows but the insectoid advanced unfazed toward the middle-aged man. It clobbered the horse's head then sliced its shins, sending the bleeding steed collapsing to the ground on top of the archer. The fallen horse struggled to get back on its feet amidst a series of panicked neighs.

As the man called desperately for it to settle down, he was set upon by two new shadow creatures. Maya's pair of casts had arrived at last.

Cylos recognized both from Belza's book. The first was a shadow hound—a mostly black canine with patches of white and brown fur, a stubby tail, and pointed ears. The second was a hopscuttle—a gray and white, furred mammalian with rabbit ears, massive paws, and buckteeth. The shadow hound clamped its teeth on the enemy's right hand, forcing him to drop his weapon with a scream, while the hopscuttle silenced him with two swift jabs to the face with its boxing-glove-like paws.

Now only two riders remained. They whipped their steeds around, readying an attack, but immediately froze at the sight of the lazzerode, mantidus, shadow hound, and hopscuttle creeping toward them in a line. They exchanged brief knowing glances.

"Let's get out of here," the woman said.

"Not worth messing with four of those things. Come on," her companion replied as they turned their horses around, digging their matching black-and-silver boots into the horses' sides, and dashed away.

Eight foes down for the count and two in retreat. Cylos could hardly believe it. It had all happened so quickly. The Montegues' four creatures hadn't been as commanding as Belza's, but they were still tremendously effective. Cylos was impressed how well the children could guide them in combat at just nine and four years old.

Soon, Zane and Maya were standing beside him, their shadow creatures returning to their sides. Maya met both her casts in a simultaneous hug, throwing an arm around each of them.

"I missed you so much," she told them, tears wetting her cheeks as the shadow hound's tail and back haunches wagged and the hopscuttle wiggled its nose.

The joyous reunion brought a smile to Cylos's face. He was thrilled he'd freed her and her brother's hands from captivity so they could use their incredible gift.

Zane was less affectionate, but stroked his lazzerode on the back once it scurried up his shoulders and patted the mantidus on the side of the head. Cylos thought of how skeptical the boy had been when they'd first met. He'd surely won his trust now.

"That was incredible. How on Tseloria did you get their gloves off?" Victor asked, interrupting Cylos's thoughts as he joined the others.

Cylos scanned the ground to find where Sharlee had discarded Belza's silver tool. He walked over to it and held it up to show Victor while wearing a wide smile on his face. "It's a long story, but a friend of mine gave this to me years ago. I'm sure he built it himself. I never knew what it was for until... well... I got a better look at the gloves and it... just kind of dawned on me."

Victor shook his head, his mouth hanging open. "Unbelievable. Now I know what took you so long to help me out. I thought you were just hiding in that log enjoying the show. But since you were busy getting their gloves off, I guess I'll let it slide," he said with a wink. He then turned to the two kids. "Nice job. Zane. Maya. You were great."

They both beamed and Zane shot him a proud thumbs up.

"You did okay, too, Cylos," Victor said with a wry grin. "But don't think for a second I didn't notice how you took the easy option going for the gimpy Sharlee and left me to face Darlos and his horse all by myself."

Cylos chuckled and threw a hand to his chest in mock indignation.

"Remind me, how did Sharlee get gimpy again? And if I remember correctly, it was the lazzerode who took Darlos out, wasn't it?"

Victor shrugged. "It all happened so fast, who can say for sure?"

They shared a laugh, then Cylos returned to more serious matters. "Maya, is your wrist okay?"

Her elation melted into a frown as she looked down at her arm to find dried blood from the cut, forgotten in all the excitement.

"It still hurts," she whined, returning her gaze to Cylos and sticking out her lower lip. "It's why I was slow to summon my casts."

Cylos smiled. "Don't worry, Maya, you were amazing and so brave. We'll get it cleaned up. Wait"—he turned to Zane—"Zane, could your panghordra do the honors?" He knew the boy would be flattered by the responsibility.

Zane stuck out his chest and smiled at Cylos, then turned toward his little sister. "Don't worry, Maya. I'll take care of you."

"While they do that, let's get the survivors tied up before they come to their senses," Victor said. "We showed those other two who retreated. I don't think they'll be coming back."

With Victor grabbing the arms and Cylos grabbing the legs of each unconscious assailant, together they dragged Yezlita, Darlos, and two others one at a time toward a couple of stout trees. With two propped up against one trunk and two against another, Victor fetched some rope from one of the sacks tied to his horse's saddle. With help from the shadow hound and lazzerode, they circled the rope around the captives and pulled it tight, eager to secure them in place before any of them came to.

Victor let out a heavy exhale and while panting said, "That won't hold them long once they wake up, but it should give us the time we need. I doubt they'll be bold enough to try a second attack anyway."

Cylos eyed the other four attackers lying dead on their impromptu battlefield, including Sharlee. He grimaced thinking about her—someone he knew personally—killed by his hand. He wished they hadn't needed to go to such measures; he hated how it felt. But when he thought back to the death of Belza and what might have happened to Victor, Zane, and Maya if they hadn't acted so decisively, he allowed himself a deep exhale to put his mind at peace.

It had taken Zane several minutes to form the challenging pang-hordra shadow symbol after dissipating his mantidus, but the squatty, long-snouted creature made quick work of Maya's wound, leaving her wrist with little more than a scratch.

Victor stepped toward the Montegue siblings and crouched down on one knee. "As fun as this has been, what do you say we get out of here and get you two to Central?"

Both Maya and Zane's eyes lit up at the mention.

"Yeah!"

"Let's go!"

Once the shadow creatures were dissipated, they mounted the two horses. Zane rode behind Victor, and Maya behind Cylos. Cylos was glad to feel Maya squeeze his waist without the cumbersome caster gloves prodding him this time. She leaned her head into him again as well. "Thank you, Cylos. For everything. I'll never forget this. Mom and Dad always told Zane and me there were more good lonrelmians than bad in the world. I'm glad you and Victor showed us that's true."

Her words had been simple yet sincere. The message they held went straight to Cylos's heart. He thought of the conversation in Belza's cabin years ago, when he told him he would no longer be satisfied with doing nothing, that he was committed to becoming a lonrelmian who actively stood up for casters, no matter the risk or sacrifice.

Maya had rekindled that desire in him, fueling his resolve to put his fear behind him for good. He was finally on the path to fulfilling what he'd promised years ago.

CHAPTER 16

EMERGENCE OF AN ADVOCATE

The view of towering white stone walls in the distance was a majestic sight.

It had been a long ride for Cylos, Victor, and the Montegues, lasting two weeks with few breaks and constant fear of facing more assailants. But with Maya and Zane's hands free and their caster beams accessible, albeit hidden to avoid suspicion, Cylos was much more confident that nothing could stop them. Fortunately, the remainder of their journey was peaceful, and with their destination now in sight, his shoulders relaxed as relief flooded over him.

When they entered the main gates of the city that Victor had explained was newly dubbed Central, Cylos couldn't believe how little he knew about the once-abandoned caster town. He was impressed to see crews of workers and endless scaffolding spread throughout the interior and exterior of the city.

The outer walls, dirty and tarnished from years of neglect, were being polished back to a smooth, resplendent white. The massive wooden gates were undergoing repairs and buildings were under construction and renovation all along the spiraling hilltop leading to the top of the city. There was an energy within the walls unlike anything Cylos had felt before, like all the people were excited to build something new together. He had no doubt that soon the new capital would be a magnificent, bustling sight. He was eager to see it filled with casters and lonrelmians alike, working together in harmony, a dream that for most of his life had been unfathomable.

Following Victor up the winding path that scaled the large hill within the white walls, they at last arrived at the city's apex where a large, rectangular building made of black metal triangles with twisting spires on each corner was getting worked on and a separate round building next to it was in the early stages of construction. Despite all the work left to do, the beginnings of the illustrious pair of buildings before him took his breath away.

"Zane! Maya!" a pair of voices exclaimed, interrupting his marveling.

As Cylos looked toward the source, he saw a man and a woman running toward them, tears streaming down their faces.

"Mom! Dad!" the Montegue siblings yelled in return.

Victor brought his horse to a stop and Cylos followed suit. He turned around and gave Maya a hand so she could step down. Her face was stained with tears before her feet touched the ground. Zane tried to act tough, but his quivering lip and moist eyes betrayed his true feelings. The family crashed into a loving embrace.

Cylos's throat tightened at the sight of the family reunited, and he fought to keep his composure as his eyes grew misty. He was happy for the Montegues and proud of himself. He'd made it. He'd finally taken action. The casters had been freed and returned to their family.

He cleared his throat twice and quickly wiped the moistness from his eyes, then he and Victor dismounted their horses. Giving the Montegues space for their reunion, they looked at one another and Cylos was surprised to see even the steely Victor Hadley with a trembling chin he attempted to mask behind a smile.

"Can you believe it, Cylos? We made it. I'm sure glad I had your help." He threw Cylos a sardonic grin. "And that I didn't accidentally kill you when we fought outside the cave."

This made Cylos laugh, helping further avoid the tears he'd been suppressing. "Yeah, I'm grateful for that too. Maybe next time ask questions before you start swinging. But I agree. I'm glad we did it together."

"So, what will you do now?"

"Well, I—"

"Victor, we can't thank you enough for bringing our children back to us safely." It was Zane and Maya's father. He had approached them along with his wife and the two children. Maya's eyes, nose, and cheeks were soaked as she clung to her mother who hugged her back tightly.

"Of course. It was an honor," Victor said.

Taking a hand off Maya only long enough to wipe a tear from either eye, Maya's mother spoke next. "I'm certain there will be more work for you soon. But before we get to that, who is your friend?" She gestured toward Cylos.

"This is Cylos. You actually have him to thank for rescuing your children more than me. We were working together in Perlatum. He's the one who got assigned the job to retrieve Zane and Maya and found them first. I thought he was going to turn them in for the reward. Little did I know, well... and I think little did he know... he was on our side all along."

Victor threw him another smile and Cylos felt his cheeks flush.

"I'm glad you were there for Victor and our children. Thank you, Cylos," the Montegues' mother said. She took a shaky breath then continued, "My name is Amelia, and this is my husband Adrian."

"It's a pleasure to meet you," Cylos responded.

Victor interjected. "You should know, Cylos is also the one who got them out of their caster gloves. You have to show them how you did that, Cylos."

Cylos felt a little sheepish, but he didn't argue as he unslung his pack and pulled out the tool from its sheath. "One of my closest friends, a caster who died years ago, gave this to me. I never knew what it was for until I looked closer at the caster gloves on Zane and Maya and figured it out. It broke the locks and released them right away." Cylos gave a brief demonstration of how it worked, then handed it over to Adrian and Amelia Montegue for inspection. He was glad he'd cleaned it during their trek.

"Impressive. I've never seen anything like this. Your friend must have invented it. This could be useful. Maybe we can recreate it to share with others," Adrian said.

"If it will help other casters, you're welcome to take it. I'm sure that's exactly what my friend would have wanted." Cylos also thought about the book and talisman he bore. He considered showing them to the Montegues as well, but something stopped him. Belza had suggested Cylos would have the wisdom to know when to use the items he'd entrusted to him. Those words had certainly rung true with the tool. He would wait until he had the same feeling of inspiration to share the other two.

"If you're willing, let us show this to others and then we'd be happy to return the original to you the next time our paths cross or we see Victor. I can tell it's meaningful to you."

"Thank you. Sounds perfect to me," Cylos responded. It *was* meaningful to him since it had come from Belza, but he was skeptical he'd get it back. He didn't know where his path would take him next, or if he and Victor would see each other again after this. But he wouldn't bother the Montegues with those details. If he never saw the tool again, knowing it had served its purpose and was now in the hands of casters who could make significant use of it was more than enough.

"If you're not in too big of a hurry," Amelia began, "there's someone who should be here any minute and I'm certain would be thrilled to meet you."

Victor shrugged. "I can wait. Cylos, I don't know how big of a hurry you're in."

Cylos was certain his parents were beside themselves with worry. They might even be assuming the worst after how much time had passed. But it'd been this long, what was a few more minutes? "No, I can wait as well. May I ask who it is?"

Adrian Montegue shot him a crooked grin. "You'll see. Just hold tight."

They exchanged pleasant conversation with one another for a few minutes longer until, emerging from the black rectangular building before them, a brown-haired man with broad shoulders approached. The moment he appeared, Cylos was impressed by the way he held himself. Something about his aura struck Cylos as commanding and noble.

"Prime Minister," Amelia Montegue cried out. "This is the boy we told you about. He's brought Zane and Maya back to us. I'd like you to meet him and his friend."

Cylos couldn't believe his ears. *The* Prime Minister Malvus Lorenzus? That explained the impression he'd just had. Cylos felt his mouth go dry in the presence of the man set to restore casting to Malgar.

The prime minister looked at the group with a comforting smile. "I'm so glad to see Zane and Maya returned," he said, before turning to the pair of teenagers. "Thank you both so much. It's Victor, isn't it?"

He nodded to show confirmation, then the prime minister turned to Cylos. "And your name?"

Cylos was tongue-tied. But after swallowing hard he managed to find the words. "My name is Cylos. Cylos Phetos." He hoped his voice hadn't quivered.

"Cylos Phetos, that's a good strong name," Lorenzus said with a pleasant grin. "I'll remember that one. Thank you for helping the Montegues. Malgar needs more young people like yourselves to stand up for what's right, especially with such exciting changes on the horizon. Soon thugs like those who captured Zane and Maya will have no chance of getting away with harming casters. It won't be long now until casters no longer need to mask their powers or hide at all. It's going to be different than before the Purge, but I believe it will be wonderful and Malgar will be better for it."

Cylos wasn't sure what was prompting Lorenzus to share all this with them. Perhaps it was gratitude for fellow lonrelmians willing to risk their own wellbeing for casters as Lorenzus had done so unabashedly throughout his political ascent. Or maybe it was mere excitement at what he was organizing. Perhaps some of both. Either way, Cylos wasn't about to complain or interrupt. Hearing this declaration from the prime minister himself gave him goosebumps.

"I'm proud to say the final piece of the puzzle has at last fallen into place. I've received word from the caster I've been waiting on. The lynchpin. Now that he's agreed to lead the Legion of Shadow Casters, I have no doubt the Lonrelmian Ministry will proceed precisely as I've proposed."

"You mean, Master Toshio?" Amelia interjected. "He's committed to it?"

Cylos didn't know who they were referring to but the excitement in her voice was palpable.

Lorenzus nodded. "Yes, I received a messenger bat from him this morning. He has accepted."

Adrian and Amelia turned to one another, wide smiles on their faces as tears started flowing anew. They put an arm around each other's shoulders and Adrian pulled Zane into his side while Maya remained with her head buried into her mom's neck.

Amelia faced Lorenzus. "At this rate, Zane and Maya will grow up under much more favorable circumstances than we did. We can't thank you enough, Prime Minister."

"Your gratitude is appreciated though unnecessary. I'm only doing what's right for shadow casters and for all Malgarians. There are many others who have sacrificed far more than I have to get us to this point."

He directed his attention back toward the teenage boys. "Victor, Cylos, there will soon be much work to do. I'm counting on you and others like you to advance this cause. I can assure you, with the reinstatement of shadow casters and the formation of LoSC—the Legion of Shadow Casters—Malgar *will* prosper again."

Victor's cool confidence was ever-present. He didn't skip a beat in responding. "You can count on us, Prime Minister."

Cylos felt the same, but with his breath taken away, he could only nod. He was astounded at all he was hearing from the prime minister. A long-held dream was coming true.

Days earlier, he'd imagined returning to his parents with a monetary fortune in hand, hoping it would make them proud. Instead, he'd be returning to tell them the wonderful news about shadow casting. It wouldn't pull them out of poverty or give them the luxurious life Cylos had begun to dream of, but he knew it would be worth far more to them than the five platinum coins. His father would be prouder of him than he would about any amount of money.

The thought brought a smile to Cylos's face, but for the first time, he realized that, more importantly than seeking his father's approval, he was proud of himself.

His father had long yearned for casters' return, but he'd never acted to make it happen. Cylos loved and respected his father, but he now realized the error in sitting back passively, wishing for the past—an error he too had made since Belza's death. At last, Cylos had taken action on his own. He'd played his part in advancing shadow casting's return. He was devoted to making sure this was only the start.

His father's stories that once felt like fairy tales, the times and circumstances the Phetos family had so longed for, were about to become reality.

"We never finished our conversation from before," Victor said, interrupting Cylos's continued thoughts of Lorenzus and LoSC.

Having said their goodbyes after visiting with the Montegues a while longer and leaving Central's apex, the duo rode their horses together at a slow trotting pace through Central's main gates and past the white stone walls surrounding the city.

"Oh?" Cylos responded, unsure what Victor was referring to.

"You know, about what you're going to do now?"

Oh that, Cylos thought. The past few weeks had been so exhilarating, so fulfilling, so rewarding. He didn't want to think about them ending. Didn't want to imagine returning to an everyday slog of work to make ends meet. At least now he'd be equipped with the courage to speak out for casters in his interactions rather than hide.

"Well, returning to work in Perlatum is off the table, that's for sure. I guess I'll head back to Wentsling, make sure my parents know I'm okay, then look for work closer to home."

Victor tilted his head to the side, throwing Cylos a narrow-eyed glance. Keeping one hand on his horse's reins, the other went to his hip. "You're telling me after what we accomplished together, you're going to go crawling back to that?"

Cylos recoiled in his saddle. "What do you mean? Do you have a different idea?"

Victor let out a noise somewhere between a scoff and a chuckle. "Are you serious right now, Cylos? How do you think I found out about the job with Krinton, got connected to the Montegues, learned about Zane and Maya? Didn't you hear the prime minister? Times are changing and there will be more opportunity than ever to stand up for what's right and make true progress in Malgar.

"For the last year I've been part of an advocacy group for shadow casters. With casting legalized, there will be no limit to what we can do to make a difference. We'll need to help change public opinion and advance the cause of LoSC. From everything I've seen of you, both in your skill and perspective, you'd be perfect for the job."

Cylos jerked his head back and blinked.

"So, what do you say, Cylos? You want to make rescues and missions like this a permanent gig? I thought we worked pretty well together, didn't you? You want to join me?"

Cylos was at a loss for words. "Y-y-you mean... Are you serious? You'd have me along? My work could be helping shadow casters? Establishing them across the world?"

Victor chuckled. "Absolutely. That's how *I* plan to spend the next few years at least. So, are you in?"

It was overwhelming to consider but an easy decision. "Yes," Cylos declared. "I'm in, Victor. I can't think of anything I'd rather do, or anyone I'd rather team up with," he added with a smile.

"That's what I like to hear. Our next meeting is on the last day of spring, about a month from now, in Torcia, just southeast of here, with the organizers of the group and a few shadow casters. Torcia's going to be an important one as LoSC gets established. Get what you need in order, then can I plan to see you there?"

"Torcia, absolutely. I'll head to Wentsling to check in with my parents and give them the good news. I'm sure they're worried about me, then I'll meet you in Torcia in a month."

"Perfect. When you get there, ask anyone you come across to direct you to the Winnitor Manor. That's where we'll be."

"Winnitor Manor. Got it," Cylos responded. Then, calculating travel time in his head, he added, "You know what, I think I have time to make a stop before I go to Wentsling. I'm going to go through Sentinalia on my way home."

Victor's eyebrows perked up. "Sentinalia? What do you want to go through that shoddy town for?"

"A friend of mine—the one who gave me the tool to remove the caster gloves—he lived there once. Told me I should visit sometime. I don't know why or what I'd be looking for, but I think I'll stop by, see what it's like."

With a shrug, Victor said, "Suit yourself. But from what I've heard of Sentinalia, I wouldn't get your hopes up too much. Although, who am I to talk? I've always been fond of Huo Quiana Village myself and thought it'd be nice to end up there. So, if you find something you like about Sentinalia, why should I criticize it?"

It was Cylos's turn to chuckle. "Huo Quiana? Where on Tseloria is that? I've never heard of it."

"I guess that tells you all you need to know," Victor concluded with his familiar wide grin. "But trust me, the scenery there is immaculate. Anyway, go do whatever you need to, Cylos. I'll do the same, then I'll see you in Torcia in about a month. Until then, my friend."

Victor extended a hand toward Cylos and Cylos gripped it firmly, looking Victor straight in the eye. He knew this was the beginning of a long and meaningful friendship. "Until then, Victor. See you soon."

Urging his horse forward, Cylos headed northwest carving a path toward Sentinalia. As he rode, his thoughts went to Belza as they so often did. After all Cylos had learned and accomplished these past weeks, he wished more than anything he could speak to Belza and that his old friend could see him now. He liked to think perhaps Belza could.

Feeling the rush of the wind as his horse raced onward, Cylos's memory went back yet again to his first time riding Belza's alcier. In that moment, he'd felt so light, so exhilarated, so full of life and hope. He was surprised to find that, though the circumstances were very different, he felt that way again.

Looking up to the sky, he said, "I'm finally doing it, Belza. What I've always dreamed of. I'm going to make a difference for casters like I said I would."

A whirlwind of unexpressed thoughts, painful and joyous memories, and overwhelming feelings hit Cylos like a wave. Before he knew it, he could feel tears streaming down his cheeks, their cold dampness against his skin accentuated by the rushing air of his sprinting horse. He swallowed hard, a choked sensation rising in his throat as he strained to get words out without his voice shaking, speaking aloud into the sky once more.

"I promise you, Belza. I promise I will make you proud."

ALSO BY JARED WOODCOX

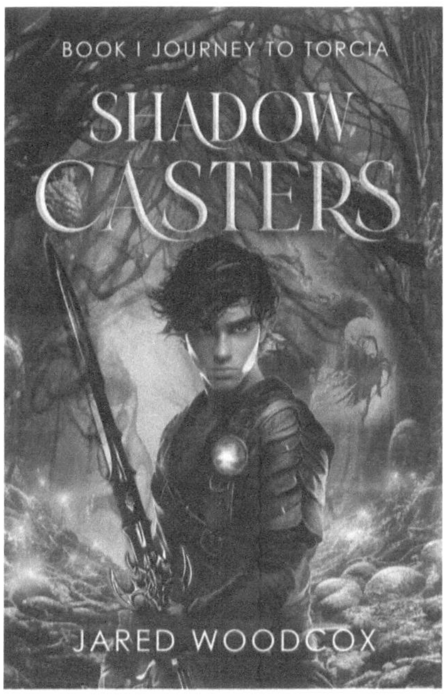

Journey to Torcia: <u>Available on Amazon</u>

"Three young casters, Kaito, Sumi, and Nigel, emerge as beacons of hope within the reinstated Legion of Shadow Casters. Together they must prove their worth in a society split by fear and prejudice.

Can Kaito, Sumi, and Nigel realize their shadow casting potential while learning to bear the weighty mantle of their new roles and withstand the crucible of their first real test?"

Defense of Huo Quiana: Available on Amazon

"They swore to uphold balance. But can they stay loyal to their cause even if it costs their lives?

Kaito, Sumi, and Nigel triumphed over their first challenge. But their troubles are only beginning . . . and when a surprise detour lands them in a distrustful town that's in grave danger, the three young casters are faced with a test that will push their resolve to its limit.

The townsfolk fear and despise them—but they also need their help.

Meanwhile, Master Toshio is plunged into a shadowy hunt to unmask a traitor lurking within the Legion of Shadow Casters. But each clue only raises more questions—and if he can't untangle the truth, their fragile organization risks collapsing back into oblivion.

The future of the shadow casters hangs in the balance. And as the trio meets new foes and discovers more about their Legion's past, they're faced with hard truths and shocking revelations that will put their deepest beliefs to the test."

ABOUT THE AUTHOR

Jared Woodcox has always been obsessed with creating. Whether it's writing songs, making up games, drawing up plays for youth sports teams he's coaching, or telling stories, his greatest joy comes from bringing something to life that didn't exist before.

Of these endeavors, none is more fulfilling than writing books such as his first published series Shadow Casters.

When not writing or dreaming up new fantasy or science fiction stories, Jared can be found spending time with his wife, son, and dog, playing guitar, or enjoying the outdoors across Colorado, Utah, and Wyoming.

Jared Woodcox

Shadow Casters Series

Shadowcasterseries.com

Visit the website for illustrations, future book information, and a glossary of terms